DON'T WALK ALONE

Mary Bringle

SCHOLASTIC INC.
New York Toronto London Auckland Sydney

For Sarah Talbot

Cover Photo by Herb Polsky

ISBN 0-590-32154-4

Published by Scholastic Book Services, a division of Scholastic Inc.

12 11 10 9 8 7 6 5 4 3 2

8 9/8 0 1 2 3/9

Printed in the U.S.A. 01

DON'T WALK ALONE

A Windswept Book

WINDSWEPT TITLES FROM SCHOLASTIC

Don't Walk Alone by Mary Bringle
Someone is Out There by Carole Standish
The Night Visitors by Miriam Lynch
The House of Three Sisters
by Virginia Nielsen McCall

One

"Don't look so glum, Amy. You might even learn to like the place!" My sister, Anne, was vainly trying to tease a smile out of me. I wanted to reassure her, but somehow that smile just wouldn't come.

"I'm sorry," I said. "I didn't know it showed."

"I've heard Northern California's beautiful," put in Doug, swerving off the turnpike and following the signs for Newark Airport. "Anyway, your father certainly seems to like it. His last letter was like something the Chamber of Commerce would put out."

We all smiled then, picturing Dad and his enthusiasms. My father, Dr. Charles Hollis, is a naturalist. Where other men might get excited over ball games or stock market reports, Daddy goes wild over rare birds or weird pine cones. He knows just about everything there is to know about nature, and I'm proud of him. The only trouble is that he moves around a lot. This new job at North Point College in California was the latest in a long line.

"You have to promise to send me pictures," said Anne. "It sounds like paradise."

She and Doug exchanged one of their small, private smiles. They looked so wonderful together, so exactly *right,* that I couldn't help but envy them a little. Anne is just seven years older than I am. At twenty-three she was married to a man she adored, had a wonderful baby boy, and was expecting another baby in four months. In fact, it was because of the new baby that we were on our way to the airport. I'd been living with Doug and Anne, completing my junior year at Brancroft High, ever since Dad moved to California. We'd all agreed it would be best for me to finish out the year and then — well, "We'll see," Dad had said. Without really dwelling on it, I guess I'd had my heart set on going to Brancroft for senior year, too.

Of course I missed Dad. I wrote to him all the time, and I'd been planning to visit him in California for the summer, but with the coming addition to my sister's family the summer visit had turned into a full-scale move. There just wasn't room in Anne's little house for five of us. Even though she would never have kicked me out, I knew I couldn't do that to them.

I studied Anne now, noticing the way the sun danced in her springy blond hair, turning it to liquid gold. With her slightly upturned nose and navy blue eyes, Anne was the picture of our mother. Sometimes I looked at photographs of Mom, who died when I was twelve, and was astonished at the resemblance. I used to wonder if Dad felt twinges of pain whenever he looked at Anne, but if he did he never showed it. He always claimed his two girls were the joy of his life. All the more reason for me to feel guilty about my reluctance to move to California!

A glimpse of my face in the rearview mirror pointed up the difference between Anne and me. While my sister had inherited golden curls, I had come out with my father's dark hair. Instead of those marvelous, deep blue eyes, mine looked back at me from beneath my level dark eyebrows and seemed to mock me with their uninteresting hazel color. Stick-straight hair which fell just to my shoulders, a straight, no-nonsense nose, and high cheekbones completed the picture.

"You have a marvelous smile, Amy. That is, when you remember to smile." That's what Miss Price, my sixth-grade teacher, had said when she was casting the Thanksgiving pageant. Marvelous smile or not, I still got to play a silent Indian that time around.

"Did you remember to pack your sketchbook and art supplies?" Anne asked from the front seat.

I nodded. That was Anne all over. Not only was she beautiful and vivacious, she really kept tabs on people. She always knew the right thing to say. She could put anybody at ease, and she did it so effortlessly. Only Anne would suggest that the prospect of having new vistas to sketch was a bonus for me. Aside from seeing Dad again, it looked like the only bonus.

From what I'd heard, Klamath Heights was miles from anywhere. There was some dinky town, Klamath, which routed the mail through, but it sounded like the kind of place where the entire high school might contain about twenty kids.

"You'll get to know everyone so much faster that way," optimistic Anne had said when I'd confided my fears.

"I'm not so sure. In those small towns everybody's known each other for *years*. Since they were born! They don't take much to outsiders." I was remembering the small town in Kentucky where Daddy had dragged us when I was ten.

"You just have to make them like you." Anne had smiled to soften the words. It was easy enough for *her*. Everybody liked Anne automatically. With me it was tougher. I got so tongue-tied around new people I could barely get a coherent sentence out. Naturally, that made them think I was stuck-up, and pretty soon word got around that that new girl, Amy Hollis, thought she was better than anybody else. Consistently getting good grades sort of reinforced the image. I seemed to have spent most of my life aching for friends but being too shy to put out the right signals. At least here, in New Jersey, I'd made a place for myself. I had several friends — junior year girls who were smart enough to see past my seemingly icy exterior and make the effort to know me.

I knew Anne thought it was strange that I'd never had a real boyfriend. When she was sixteen they were running after her in swarms. Once I overheard her telling Doug that it was because Mom had died when I was twelve. "She's more comfortable with adults than kids her own age," she'd said. "It's partly Dad's fault for treating her like a grown-up."

I suppose he did, in his way. It wasn't that he didn't care about me, or worry. Daddy just couldn't keep his mind on any one thing long enough to help me when I needed him. We'd be discussing whether or not I could stay out until eleven o'clock on a Saturday and suddenly, right in the middle of it, he'd start thinking about some rare ferns out in the Great Swamp of New Jersey or something. You couldn't get mad at him, though. He's just too lovable. I know he should marry again and settle down with another woman he could love. But I doubt that will happen. Anne says Daddy was a One-Man Woman. Some men are just that way.

"Here we are," said Anne. "Newark Airport! Next stop — San Francisco."

"And then a hundred mile drive up the coast to the boonies," I added glumly.

"That's just an example of what I've been trying to tell you," Anne sighed. "You mustn't be so negative. Amy, honey, give it a chance."

"You're right," I said. "You're always right. I just wish I could be more like you."

Doug smiled. "You're your own girl, Amy. I think you'll do just fine." Then he turned to get my luggage out of the trunk.

Tears blurred my eyes as I hugged them both good-bye, but I blinked them back and forced a big smile. I even tried to put some bounce in my step as we strode along toward the departure gate. After all, I didn't want to seem negative.

The last glimpse I had of them was typical. They were waving for all they were worth, standing close together, and holding hands. Anne's baby was just beginning to show. I'd never seen her looking lovelier, or more radiant. "Lucky Anne," I whispered to myself "You know where you're going. You've found what you want in life."

I was sixteen and a half, and I wondered if I'd ever know what it was like to feel so secure and happy. As I boarded the plane, I said a quick goodbye to that leafy, green town in New Jersey where I'd begun to feel at home. From now on, home would be Klamath Heights, California. Even the name sounded cold and remote.

Somewhere over the Grand Canyon I must have fallen asleep, because the next thing I knew the little light for the seatbelts was on and we had begun the descent toward San Francisco Airport. I shouldn't have fallen asleep — I wasn't tired, really — but I have this tendency to go to sleep whenever I don't feel like facing the future.

I had been engaging in my favorite fantasy. My only fantasy, I should say. It would embarrass me to tell anyone about it, and I'd never confided in anyone back in New Jersey. Not even my two best friends, and certainly not Anne. How could a sixteen-and-a-half-year-old girl admit to having invented an ideal boyfriend who seemed more real than flesh-and-blood boys?

I guess I made him up during my sophomore year. Lots of the other girls were dating, and a few were already going steady. Since I clammed up automatically whenever a boy tried to make conversation with me,

I wasn't exactly a candidate for most popular girl. When I was alone I'd imagine all the bright, funny replies I could have made, but that didn't do any good when it came to real encounters. Gradually, I dreamed up this ideal person. He was gentle and had a soft, deep voice, and whenever I was with him I knew exactly what to say. I never felt shy, or tongue-tied, or goofy with him. He made me laugh, the way I'd seen girls do at Brancroft High when they were walking down the halls, kind of tilting their heads up sideways and crinkling their eyes at the corners. He could be serious, too. We spent a lot of time talking about our futures, discussing what kinds of music we liked, and debating about whether I should go to an art school or major in art at a regular college.

I even knew what he looked like — tall, with dark, curling hair and blue eyes. He had a slow, lazy, kind of lopsided grin. The only thing I didn't give him was a name. I had an almost superstitious feeling that if I named him he'd go away, vanish from my fantasy life.

It was because I'd been imagining talking to him, on the flight to San Francisco, that I fell asleep. I felt odd and lost when I woke up — sort of caught between two worlds and belonging in neither. All that changed when we landed at the airport. There was too much to do all at once. I was caught up in the flow of all those people streaming toward the main terminal, and before I had a chance to even look for my luggage I saw my father coming toward me, smiling.

It always amazed me to realize that my father was a very good-looking man. To me he was just

Daddy, but when I saw him unexpectedly, like this, I felt a little jolt of pride. He's tall and long-legged, like me, and his dark hair falls over his forehead in a floppy way that makes you want to push it back. Today he was wearing a tweedy kind of jacket and pants that looked suspiciously like blue jeans.

He caught me up in a big hug, and I smelled the familiar odor of pipe tobacco and the bay rum he always uses after shaving. I hugged back, hard, realizing how much I'd missed him. "Hello, *Sciurus carolinensis*," he said. "I can't tell you how good it is to see you." The Latin meant squirrel, which had always been his pet name for me. When you're the daughter of a naturalist, you get used to things like that.

The drive from San Francisco started off well enough. We had a million things to tell each other, and it was a beautiful, golden day. The sun had a different quality than back east, or maybe I'd just heard too many songs about California sunshine. Anyway, I was suddenly filled with the most wonderful, peaceful feeling. As if reading my mind, my father turned and smiled at me.

"I think you're going to like it here, honey," he said. "I know it's a big change for you, but if you'll give it a chance you'll find it grows on you."

"Is it at all like the town we just passed?"

"Oh, no. Klamath Heights is much smaller, Amy. The coast is quite rugged farther up, and there's a wonderful view of the sea from our cottage."

"What's Crozier's Cottage like? I picture white picket fences and rose gardens when I hear the word 'cottage.' "

Daddy threw back his head and roared. "You

have quite a surprise in store then, squirrel. There isn't a white picket fence within miles of Klamath, and the climate isn't right for roses."

"What's it right for?" I should have known better. For the next fifteen minutes my father treated me to a detailed description of the flora and fauna surrounding our new home. Complete, of course, with Latin names. "You'll be dying to sketch some of the trees along the coast road. They're bent into fantastic shapes, because of the high winds during the winter. You've never seen anything like it."

The image of the trees, buffeted and gnarled by icy winds, didn't exactly comfort me. It sounded bleak, unfriendly. What I really wanted to know about was mundane stuff like how many kids went to high school there.

"Wait and see," Daddy said. "I want you to take your impressions with your eyes, not from what I say."

We stopped at a little place for lunch, and then Dad let me drive for the next thirty miles or so. I'd just gotten my license six months ago, and I was delighted to get a chance to navigate strange roads. When we'd gone about eighty miles in all, Daddy insisted on taking the wheel again. "For the last twenty miles the roads are tricky," was all he said.

He wasn't kidding. We began to drive directly above the sea, and the road was so full of hairpin turns it made me dizzy. For long periods of time we seemed to be climbing steadily upward, with sudden brilliant flashes of sea to our left. Then, just as suddenly, we'd veer away across scrubby, gray-green terrain and the water would be lost to sight. Just when I thought we had gone deep inland, we'd find ourselves parallel to the ocean again. I had a vision of the coast as you'd see it on a map — a wriggling, snaky line carved out by the ceaseless beating of the Pacific Ocean against the rocks.

"Look quick," my father said. "You won't see it again for a while." I had a brief view of a lighthouse, slim and blinding white. Soaring cliffs of forbidding gray rock loomed beyond it. It was a beautiful setting, but like the misshapen, wind-bent trees, not exactly homey.

The road plunged directly down and really did go inland this time. Soon we were on the outskirts of Klamath, a pretty town nestled in a valley that was covered with pine trees. Small frame buildings lined the street. There were the usual grocery stores and pharmacies, a three-story courthouse, and a movie theater. There was also a clapboard building called the Timber Tavern which advertised the best pizza in town. As far as I could see, it was the *only* pizza in town.

"Was that it?" I asked. "Was that all there is to Klamath?"

"Most of the people live out along the lake," my father said. "The school you'll be going to is out there, too."

The lake, I had to admit, looked super. It was a deep, spring-fed lake of an incredible blue, ringed with pines and birches. I could see about a dozen kids my age sunning on the small beach or swimming out toward a raft. The roofs of the houses Dad had mentioned could just be seen poking up above the thick foliage.

The school was something else again. For some reason it reminded me of a model prison. Unlike anything else in Klamath, it was gleaming and modern. At least, I thought, all that red brick seemed to say that there were several hundred students at Klamath High.

"Of course the school serves all the rural areas around here," said Dad, unknowingly dashing my hopes. "There can't be more than twenty kids your age in Klamath itself." He beamed, as if this would please me. I opened my mouth to say something, but I heard my sister's voice warning me not to be negative, so I shut it again.

We had circled the little lake by now. Abruptly, the road took us on another upward spiral, and soon we were back in that bleak, gray-green world again. The pines and birches vanished, and all that remained was the scrubby grass that grows near the sea, punctuated by an occasional, tormented-looking tree.

"Only five miles from Klamath to Klamath Heights," Daddy said cheerfully. Heights was right. I had the uncomfortable feeling that we were approaching the forbidding cliffs again. Once I even thought we might drive straight off the edge of the world, because I could sense the sea without seeing it. Daddy took a sharp left, just when it seemed we couldn't go any higher, and there it was — the ocean. The sight of so much water spread out below us almost took my breath away. It seemed to fill the whole horizon, vast and blue.

"Do we live up here?" I whispered, clutching my hands together so hard they ached.

"On the cove." Now there was a deep descent between hills covered with gorse and the road turned into little more than a track. It was pitted and rough, and we jolted along right up to a gray post with a sign that said: CROZIER'S COTTAGE — PRIVATE. Down the path was a great gray hulk of a house perched crazily on a bluff above the sea. I couldn't see any cottage, and just as I was about to ask, my father smiled with pride and pleasure and said: "We're home, squirrel."

I squinted my eyes for a better look, but the light from the water was almost blinding. Daddy took my bags and we approached on foot, crunching over a gravel path hemmed in by weeds. My father murmured something about having to start in on the gardening, but I couldn't reply. I was too stunned by the sight of my new home to do anything but stare.

Whoever had built Crozier's Cottage certainly didn't have picket fences in mind. It looked to me as if someone had slapped two wings on to the central part while they were wearing a blindfold — one side of the house actually seemed ready to fall into the ocean. The wood had weathered to a peculiar, no-color gray, which looked almost silver where the sun struck. Like a welcoming committee, a huge white sea gull was sitting squarely on the slate-tiled roof. The windows were small and reminded me of jack-o'-lantern eyes — warm and mellow when the candle is lit, but dead and dark otherwise. I had the peculiar feeling that there was nothing inside, that you could step into Crozier's Cottage and fall straight into the sea.

"Well, Amy? What do you think of it?"

"It's very unusual," I said in a small voice.

"Wait until you see the cove. It's perfect for swimming."

I smiled at him, hoping he couldn't tell I'd taken an instant dislike to the place. I couldn't even imagine what it might be like to swim here, along this forbidding coast. The bluffs to the north were gentle, rising in rounded humps from the sea. Each hump was a little larger than the next, until, as if it were a trick to fool unwary strangers, the pretty coast turned savage. The cliffs I had seen from the road reared up sheer from the sea, protected at their base by black, jagged rocks. There was nothing gentle about them.

My father had said the place would grow on me, but I couldn't ever imagine feeling at home here. In fact, it seemed to me that Crozier's Cottage must be the loneliest place in the world. The thought made me shiver, even though the sun was warm and bright.

The gull that had been sitting on the roof went flapping off, giving an eerie screech, and I followed my father up the path to the door.

Three

The inside of the cottage wasn't exactly reassuring, but it was less forbidding than the outside. There was so much to see and explore, so many odd little nooks and unexpected spaces, that my natural curiosity took over. I don't think my father even sensed that rush of uneasiness, fear, almost, I'd registered at first sight of the house. He rushed around the place, proudly pointing out features he was sure I'd like.

"Just look at this fireplace, Amy! Isn't it a beauty?" The fireplace, in the cavernous living room, was an enormous old slate-floored thing with flagstones all around it leading up to a rough wooden mantelpiece. I could imagine it blazing away cheerfully on a cold winter night, but right now it just looked like a yawning, empty mouth. The furniture was heavy and dark, too, although it looked comfortable enough. The total impression of the room would have been dismal enough without the framed prints over the mantel. Each one showed a shipwreck, tall masts splintered like toothpicks, broken hulls thrusting up at crazy angles, smashed against jagged rocks. "Hope you brought your sketchbook, squirrel," Daddy said, as if reading my mind. "Plenty to work with here."

I determined then and there to do some cheerful watercolors as soon as possible. If the shipwreck prints were any indication, the house could use them. There was one lovely feature of the living room, and that was the long, curving window seats built into the bay windows facing the sea. They were broad enough to lie on, and I could imagine reading or sketching there, drowsing away lazy afternoons with the whole blue expanse of the Pacific at my elbow. From here I could see the little cove my father had mentioned. It was a white crescent of sugary-looking sand, lapped by blue waves, and it looked safe and protected. The angle of the house blocked the view of the jagged cliffs, and it was possible to imagine that the entire coast was as gentle and pretty as Crozier's Cove.

"Come and see the rest, Amy." Daddy was anxiously leading the way, pointing out the fine, carved edges on the big bowfront chest in the dining room, leading me up a funny little half-flight of stairs to a book-lined room destined to be his library. It was presided over by a stuffed seabird whose glass eyes looked distinctly unfriendly.

"*Haliaeetus albicilla,*" my father said, as if introducing us.

The kitchen was the cheeriest room in the house, with its broad work counters, hanging copper pots, and scrubbed oak table. Stairs led up from the kitchen to the second story, but they were dark and splintery. The main staircase was lit by a fan-shaped window on the first landing — the little semicircular shape was bright blue, as if the sea swirled behind it, reminding me of a porthole. My own bedroom, down the hall from Daddy's, was large and light and pretty. My father had bought a red-and-green-striped down comforter that made the bed looked warm and inviting, and I was admiring it when a sound came shrieking through the house that made my spine stiffen with horror. It was a high, despairing scream, like that of a howling banshee, and it filled every room of Crozier's Cottage, seeming to swell and come closer before it disappeared. I must have jumped visibly, because my father chuckled and slung his arm around my shoulder. "Don't worry, Amy. A seabird was calling down the chimney, that's all. The sound is magnified by the stone and reverberates. You ought to hear it in the fireplace."

"No, thanks," I whispered. From the little dormer window I could see the ocean below, and with a feeling of dread I allowed my eyes to sweep up the coast. It was just as I'd feared. My bedroom was in a wing of the house that provided an excellent view of the jagged cliffs. They seemed to mock me by their very presence, and I drew the little white chintz curtains over the window and shivered. It was cold in the house, even in summer, and the thought of what it might be like six months from now was almost too depressing to contemplate.

"Well, what do you think?" My father was smiling eagerly, anxious for me to set my seal of approval on our new home. "It's a wonderful house,"

I said, smiling as I lied. "I think it might take a little getting used to, though."

"Exactly," he beamed. "Why, in a week or so you won't even notice the sea gulls crying."

I discovered I was more tired from my trip than I'd imagined, because not long after we had a makeshift supper — soup from the stock of cans in the cupboards, and peanut butter sandwiches — I began to feel drowsy. Daddy insisted I walk around to the back of the house and watch the panoramic late sunset over the ocean. I guess I'm glad he did, because it was one of the most gorgeous sights I'd ever seen. On my first night, it took my breath away and even later I could hardly believe the beauty of it.

The sky was streaked with bands of red and purple, and each band was outlined in fiery gold. The sea, quiet now, reflected the gold so that the calm ripples seemed to have caught fire, and then slowly, slowly, the blazing colors dimmed and the sun dipped below the horizon as if it had fallen into the sea. The sky turned from a no-color gray to a deep blue, and the only sound in the approaching night air was the ceaseless surge of the water, comforting now, like a lullaby.

"Thank you," I whispered, overcome by an emotion I didn't quite understand. "It was beautiful. I wouldn't have missed it for the world."

I went to bed soon after, and even in that unfamiliar room, beneath my new down comforter, my body felt warm and relaxed. Occasionally I could hear a gull crying, far away over the water, and always the soft sighing of the ocean. Before I knew it, I had sunk into a deep and dreamless sleep, my first at Crozier's Cottage. The last clear thought I had was that maybe, just maybe, things would be all right here after all.

The feeling was still with me when I woke early the next morning. Sun was pouring through the little dormer window and the sky was so bright it was everywhere. I dressed quickly and went down to the kitchen. My father was still asleep. I found some tea bags in the cupboards, and a bowl of fresh oranges stood on the table. I boiled water for the tea and squeezed two glasses of fresh juice, and then I sat down and made a list of all the things we needed to buy in Klamath. It made me feel useful, and purposeful, and I was sorry when I'd finished. I could see that time would be my greatest enemy at Crozier's Cottage until school began. The day stretched ahead endlessly, with nothing but the trip to town to break it up, and I was beginning to feel depressed again when I heard my sister's voice warning me not to be negative. "Right, Annie," I murmured. There were books to read and pictures to sketch and, when I got up the nerve to brave the cold-looking water, a cove to swim in. Plenty of things to do.

It wasn't until we drove into town that the good feeling began to disappear. The trip started off fine, and my father and I were both in high spirits. The sun was high in the sky and it gilded everything with golden light. Even the tormented-looking trees seemed to sparkle and gleam. The lake in Klamath, seen from the hill, looked like a giant, sunken sapphire. My heart started beating unreasonably hard when we parked the car on the tiny main street. Today I'd be going into the stores; I might meet people my age whom I'd be seeing in school next fall. I felt both nervous and elated.

Our first stop was the market, where I piled our cart so full of things my father protested laughingly. "This is enough to last us all summer," he said. The girl behind the cash register was tall and tanned and seemed to be about my age. Her long, efficient fingers swept our items along the counter impatiently. She gave my father a small, polite smile, but when her eyes met mine she looked down quickly, frowning. I told myself she might be shy, but just then two boys passed by on the street outside and she gave them a radiant smile and waved. "Going swimming?" one of them mouthed, and she mouthed back "Later!" I felt a stab of envy then. They seemed so carefree and easygoing.

"Come on, *sciurus,*" my father said, hefting three bursting bags of groceries. I felt myself blush and looked to see if the girl had heard, but she seemed a million miles away. She was twirling a strand of long, streaky blond hair and staring out the window.

At the drugstore it was even worse. Three girls came in, wearing cut-offs and shirts knotted at their waists. They were talking and laughing as they came through the door, but when they saw me they stopped dead. One of them stared at me openly, and I wanted to drop through the floor. For one thing, they were all so tall and tanned I felt almost like a midget. You didn't have to look at me more than once to know I didn't belong here. I had "outsider" stamped all over me. For another thing, I was getting the distinct impression that the kids of Klamath were every bit as clannish and closed-off to strangers as I had feared.

When I tried to explain this to my father, he scoffed gently. We were at the Timber Tavern, having some of their famous pizza for lunch, and he asked me what was wrong.

"I don't expect them to fall all over me," I said. "It wouldn't be natural — they don't even know who I am. But they don't have to stare at me as if I'd just dropped in from Saturn."

"Don't be so sensitive, Amy. You're imagining things. I've been told the young people here are a friendly lot."

"Who told you that?"

"Professor Herman, for one. He teaches at North Point, but he and his family live in Klamath. He has a daughter your age. Miranda, I think, is her name. The Hermans have invited us to dinner in a few days. Miranda is very anxious to meet you."

"Well," I said grudgingly, "that's nice." I forced down another wedge of pizza, trying not to notice the tall, blond boys who were idling around the jukebox and sending inquisitive looks our way. More Klamath giants, I thought.

"Bill Herman told me his daughter is involved in all sorts of activities at school. She's very popular." He reached across the table and squeezed my hand. "Don't worry, squirrel. She'll show you the ropes."

When we drove back to the cottage with our carload of supplies I had an unwelcome thought. I'd been stupid to insist on buying so much. Now we wouldn't have an excuse to go shopping again for days. While my father went to his library to work on a paper, I unpacked the groceries, lingering as long over the task as I could. Then I went out back and looked dubiously at the little protected cove. Certainly it was secluded and inviting, but, try as I might, I just couldn't convince myself that the water was warm enough to swim in. Far up the coast, the outline of the cliffs seemed to cast a shadow over the inlet, and even the hint of that shadow was enough to make me shiver.

Four

Looking back, that first week at Crozier's Cottage seems to have lasted for a year. The days were endless, each one sunnier and more beautiful than the last, and I kept thinking how perfect they might have been if only there'd been someone to share them with; someone my own age. Isolated as we were, I sometimes felt my father and I were the only people left in the world.

Several times I took the car and did the shopping in Klamath, after promising Daddy that I'd drive carefully and mind the hairpin curves. Each time I walked along the little main street I felt lonelier than ever. The blond giants, as I'd come to think of them secretly, stared right through me whenever we happened to pass on the sidewalk or found ourselves in the same store. Once I thought a girl was smiling at me and I felt ridiculously grateful. I was about to smile back, feeling that same paralyzing shyness that used to grip me back in Brancroft High, when she walked right past me. I heard her whispering and giggling with another girl, who was lounging by the cosmetics counter, and felt sure they were talking about me. When I got back home I found my father squinting through his binoculars out in back of the cottage.

"Look, squirrel," he breathed excitedly. "This is a rare one."

I took the binoculars and tried to get all worked up over the seabird he was pointing out at the edge of the cove, but there was something more important I wanted to know.

"Daddy? When are we going to that professor's house for dinner?"

His face registered a blank, so I jogged his memory a little. "The one who has a daughter? Miranda?"

"Oh, yes," he murmured, adjusting the binoculars and training them further out to sea. "I don't exactly remember, Amy. I've got it written down in my memo book."

I suppressed a sigh. Wonderful as my father was, he could be infuriating at times. Ask him the name of any plant, tree, or blade of grass within twenty miles and he'd reply promptly, but something like a dinner date in Klamath escaped his mind completely.

"The thing is," I continued awkwardly, "maybe I wouldn't have to go with you. I'm sure this Miranda doesn't care about meeting me. If she's anything like the kids I see in town I know we'd have nothing in common."

"You've spoken to them, then?" He put down the binoculars and gave me all his attention.

"No, but — "

"Well, then, how can you know you have nothing in common?" he asked reasonably.

"Because they don't *want* to know me. They don't want to speak to me." I knew I sounded childish, but there was nothing I could do about it.

"Maybe," said my father, with irritating logic, "that's what they think about *you*."

It was useless. I headed for the house when he called me back. "I know what I wanted to tell you," he said. "I've finally hired a housekeeper. She'll start next Monday, and I think you'll find her very pleasant. She's from Klamath, of course, and she seems competent and friendly. During the summer she'll be coming three times a week, but once you're in school and I'm up at North Point she'll come every day."

I wanted to tell him there was no need for a housekeeper, at least not yet. My little duties around the place helped to pass the time, and without them I wondered what I'd find to do, but then I reconsidered. At least a housekeeper was someone to talk to, another human being around Crozier's Cottage instead of my father and me alone with every sea gull on the Pacific coast.

"Her name is Mrs. Morgan, I believe."

"You believe? Don't you know?"

"I've got it written down," said my father. He was so unaware of how comical it sounded I wanted to hug him, but then he had sighted another seabird and he was a million miles away. I decided to go for a swim, and went up to my room to get the bright red suit Anne and I had picked out at Crowell's Department Store a few weeks ago.

"Now *this,*" Anne had crowed, "might have been made for you! With a little tan and your black hair you'll be the siren of the Pacific."

I remembered her words as I pulled the suit on and studied myself in the mirror. Siren of the Pacific, indeed! My slinky red suit was destined to be admired only by the beady eyes of gulls. Still, I had to admit I looked pretty good. I was still very slender, but some of the sharp bones had miraculously been smoothed away, and where there had been only angles last year, there were gentle curves now. My legs seemed impossibly long, but that, according to Anne, was something to be thankful for. I shoved my feet into sandals and was about to slip into my terry robe when something made me stand very still and alert, listening. There was no actual sound, nothing I could pinpoint, but suddenly I didn't feel alone anymore. Gooseflesh swept over my bare legs and arms in a wave of pure cold sensation, and then I called out: "Who's there?" The sound of my voice frightened me. How long I stood there I don't know, but gradually I became aware of the sound of the front door opening and heard my father whistling as he went to his study.

The fear passed then, but the odd feeling of being watched wasn't entirely new. Ever since coming to Crozier's Cottage there were moments when the silence thickened slightly and I had the distinct impression that something was wrong — not horribly wrong, exactly, but weird. It was like looking at one of those pictures we had when we were little. "Can you tell what's wrong in this picture?" the label would read, and then you'd look and find it was something silly and harmless. A woman sitting with her feet beneath a table would be wearing mismatched shoes, or a cat sleeping by a hearth would have no tail. That was how I'd felt ever since the first day, without putting it into words. Today was the first time I'd felt fear — cold, heavy, and paralyzing. I grabbed my robe and ran down the stairs and out the door, grateful to be in the sunlight once more.

The cove was reached by a long, crazy flight of steps which had been cut into the side of the little bluff. Each step had slats of wood gridded over the surface to keep you from slipping, but the steps were different sizes and it was necessary to go carefully. A neat border of stones, painted white, wound along beside the steps, but the grass was overgrown and some of the white markers were entirely covered over. Toward the bottom the grass disappeared, and there were only huge boulders to the right and left.

I emerged in a world so lovely and entrancing it took my breath away. From up above, the cove had looked inviting enough, but here, at its edge, it was a miniature paradise. The little half-moon of white sand was ringed round with shells and stones of every imaginable color and shape. There were shells as delicate and pink as a baby's ear, and great, curled white ones that gleamed like pearls in the sea light.

There were striped stones in colors like pale sherbet and velvety black rocks with odd white markings, and there, beyond the magical crescent, the ocean surged in blue-green billows, hissing as it kissed the shore. Occasionally there would be a larger wave, and then the water would break in hundreds of white, creamy bubbles like the points on a perfect lemon meringue pie.

I left my sandals and robe on the sand and ran straight in, hurling myself out over a billow and under the water. It was cold, but with a warmer current beneath, and it felt delicious. I stroked out, feeling my arms cut the water clean as knives. Sea-birds swooped above me and here, where they belonged, I liked the look of them. One bobbed down on the wave next to me, regarding me curiously, and then flapped off.

To my left I could look up the coast and see the waves breaking against the base of the dizzying cliffs, but here, in Crozier's Cove, I felt as protected as an enchanted princess in her own domain. I turned over on my back and floated, feeling the sun warming my face and the water buoying me up. Our cottage peered down at me, a crazy, rambling house perched so near the edge of the bluff it seemed on its way down to meet me. From this viewpoint it looked comical, and almost friendly.

Without even meaning to, my mind was summoning up the Ideal Boy again. I hadn't thought of him since falling asleep on the way here, but I knew instinctively why I needed him now. It was so perfect here, so beautiful, I desperately wanted someone to share the joy of it with me. I knew just how he'd look when he bobbed up from beneath a wave. His dark curly hair would be plastered down on his forehead by seawater, and he would be sleek and quick as a seal. His blue eyes would reflect the color of the water and the sky, and when he laughed his teeth would show white and strong in his tanned face. We would laze around on our backs, floating and not needing to talk much, and then, at our own private signal, turn and swim for shore. I thought of how his hand would feel in mine when we ran back to the sand, of how he'd rub my hair dry with a towel and point out unusual shells. He'd find a smooth, flat rock for us to sit on, and then maybe I'd tell him about the sketch I intended to do of the cove.

Sighing, I turned and swam back to shore. In spite of the warmth of the sun I felt a little shiver pass over me, and when I put my robe on I pretended that *he* would be waiting for me at the top of the bluff. He'd be building a fire in the cottage, and when he turned to look at me the warmth in his eyes would light up the room. A part of me knew that my fantasy was childish and felt a little ashamed, but the other part didn't care. The imaginary boy was the only one who understood me completely, the only one who could share my pleasure in the beauty of the cove with its dreamy patch of ocean. Without sharing pleasure and happiness, how can you really appreciate anything?

Just as I was crunching over the shells toward the steps in the bluff, it happened again. I felt someone was watching me. This time, though, I wasn't afraid. It was as if I'd been dreaming of *him* for so long he'd become a reality. He was there, now, keeping me safe.

It wasn't until I was entering the cottage that it struck me. *Safe from what?*

Five

The Hermans lived in a big white house set on a hill above the lake, in Klamath. It was the sort of house I'd always wanted to live in — pretty, comfortable, and conventional. As we parked in front of the drive, which was lined with Norwegian pines, I felt the familiar butterflies in my stomach. My father took it for granted that Miranda Herman was just dying to have me for a friend.

Miranda opened the door for us, and the moment I saw her, I knew it wasn't true. Her smile was polite but aloof. She was tall and curvy and had the longest, silkiest blond hair I'd ever seen. It fell nearly to her waist and moved with every toss of her head like a golden mane.

"Hello, Professor Hollis," she said. "Hello, Amy. Won't you come in?" She led the way to the living room, where her parents sat sipping cocktails in front of a picture window that looked down on the lake. Professor Herman was about my father's age, though not as handsome; he and Mrs. Herman seemed genuinely nice. There was nothing appraising in their eyes, whereas Miranda had already taken in my long, patchwork skirt and blue blouse and decided they were hopeless. She herself was wearing jeans and a lavender T-shirt. She made me look overdressed and underdeveloped by comparison.

"How are you settling in at Crozier's Cottage?" Mrs. Herman asked.

My father answered enthusiastically, but the next time the question was aimed at me. "You must miss your friends. What have you been doing with yourself, Amy?"

"I swim in the cove a lot," I answered.

"Oh, but you should come swim at the lake," said Miranda. "It's much nicer."

"Amy has been sketching," said my father. "We've gone up on the bluffs to the north of the cottage and she's made a very nice start on some pictures."

"You're an artist?" Professor Herman's booming voice caught me off guard. I knew he meant well, but Miranda's cool green gaze seemed to paralyze me.

"Not really," I said. "I just fool around a little."

Miranda smiled. "The art teacher at school will be glad to have you," she said. "She has a hard time finding anyone who's interested." Outwardly, Miranda's words were friendly, but it was obvious to me she thought artists were boring.

When we were eating dinner, things got worse. Mrs. Herman suggested that Miranda could introduce me to some of the kids I'd be going to school with in the fall, and Miranda grinned and said vaguely she'd be glad to. I noticed she didn't invite me to come swimming at the lake, though, or name a time, and I would rather have choked on my roast beef than ask her. While Professor Herman and my father discussed the botany department at North Point College and Mrs. Herman told me about her older daughter, who was off in San Francisco, Miranda and I kept a polite illusion of friendliness. I've noticed something about adults — they never realize when one kid is giving another the cold treatment. When Miranda asked me if I'd bought my long skirt in New Jersey, Mrs. Herman smiled encouragingly as if we were having a fashion discussion. It never occurred to her that her daughter was subtly telling me my outfit was creepy.

After dinner, Mrs. Herman suggested that Miranda show me her room. Obediently, we trudged up the stairs in total silence. Miranda's room was like Miranda herself, casually elegant and beautiful. She had a king-size bed covered with a bright lavender and crimson spread, an enormous dressing table with more bottles and jars crowding its surface than I'd ever seen, and her own color television and bright red phone. Her closets were huge. A thick lavender carpet stretched from wall to wall. I noticed a framed photo of a good-looking boy on her bedside table, and I was just thinking that I might have seen him in Klamath when she caught the direction of my glance and smiled.

"That's Chip Lawson, my steady boyfriend. He's president of our class." She flopped on her bed and regarded me with those chilly, grape-green eyes. "Did you have a steady back east?"

"Nobody special," I murmured. Nobody at all was more like it.

Her smile curved more deeply. "The trouble is," she said in a sweet voice, examining her nails, which were polished palest pink, "in a small town like this, all the good guys are already taken. I've been going with Chip for six weeks. The most popular people in our class all go steady." She shrugged. "Of course, there are always the *others.*" She made the "others" sound like social outcasts so repulsive that no one in her right mind would want to date them.

"To tell you the truth," I said in my iciest tones, "I don't much care." Miranda arched one exquisite brow and was about to reply when her phone rang. She picked it up, turning her back on me, and cooed hello. It was Chip, her boyfriend, and for the next fifteen minutes I sat politely, trying not to listen to their conversation, which was impossible.

". . . Nobody special," said Miranda. "Just some colleague of my father's and his daughter. Tomorrow? I have to have my hair trimmed in the morning." She giggled. It was an intimate sound and I wondered what Chip had said. I felt a sharp stab of envy. Miranda didn't have to fantasize — she had a living, breathing boyfriend, someone who called her and made her laugh and held her in his arms. I looked at Chip's photograph again. He had a square chin and really, if you looked hard, kind of small eyes, eyes that didn't seem capable of much humor or kindness. My friend was much nicer looking, even if he didn't really exist. *Will you listen to yourself?* I thought. *You're getting really weird, Amy Hollis.*

When it was time to go home I was more than

ready. I thanked the Hermans and made a grateful exit with my father. It was the longest night I could remember, and I didn't want it to last a second longer.

"Well, how'd it go?" asked my father as we drove back to the Heights. He seemed to be under the impression that I'd had a terrific time, and I couldn't bear to disillusion him when he seemed to be in such high spirits. "She seems like a nice girl," he said.

"Oh, very."

He reached across and squeezed my hand. "Things are going to be just fine," he said. "You'll see."

That night, as I lay in bed, I summoned up the image of my friend. His grin was a little teasing tonight, and he told me that yes, Miranda Herman was very attractive, but he'd always preferred brunettes. Just as I was drifting off to sleep, I heard a long, mournful sound that jolted me back to wakefulness. It sounded like the bellow of an injured animal moaning in pain. For a moment I thought I'd imagined it, but it came again, filling me with dread. It wasn't until I'd calmed myself down enough to use my head that I figured out what it was, and then I nearly laughed out loud. It was only the foghorn up the coast. The weather must have turned. Miranda and Chip wouldn't be able to go to the lake, after all.

The next morning I woke up to a white world like something from a fairy tale. The fog was so thick at my window that I couldn't see the cove, and it swirled around Crozier's Cottage in thick, pale clouds. The foghorn was still bellowing away, and when I went downstairs for breakfast the air in the kitchen was cold and clammy. I built a fire in the living room, but nothing really seemed to banish the melancholy atmosphere the fog had created.

It burned off around noon, leaving the day clear but sunless. The sky, which had been so pure and blue, was gray, and the sea was gray, too. The waves lapping the cove were covered with whitecaps. It seemed impossible that only a few days earlier I had been swimming there so happily. I put on a heavy parka and, taking my sketchbook, went down the steps toward the sea. I selected a large, smooth boulder and made myself as comfortable as I could. The wind had died down and I was able to sketch without weighing the pages down with rocks, but now I had a more serious problem. It seemed there was nothing I really wanted to draw. I flipped through the halfhearted attempts I'd made on walks with my father. Here was a view of the coast, seen from the northern bluffs. I'd captured some of the savage quality of those cliffs, but there was no hint of the beauty of it, only the bleakness. My attempts at sketching the cove were equally uninspiring.

Listlessly, I picked up my pencil and began to draw. I didn't even know what I wanted to accomplish, but I knew I was tired of drawing scenes without people. My fingers worked quickly, and almost before I knew it my own image began to emerge on the paper. There was my face, solemn, unsmiling, my level eyes and dark, uninteresting hair blowing slightly in the breeze. The eyes were sad, lonely, and I made them more so, until the face staring up at me was almost a mask of tragedy. "Self-portrait showing self-pity," I wrote along the bottom of the page, and then, impatient with myself,

I snapped the book shut and gave up drawing for the day.

When I got back to the cottage, I could hear voices in the living room. I found my father talking to a middle-aged woman wearing a blue smock and worn carpet slippers. She had dark hair, curly and streaked with gray, and snapping eyes behind horn-rimmed glasses. She smiled when she saw me, but although her smile was friendly enough it didn't seem the smile of a happy woman.

"Amy," said my father. "This is Mrs. Morgan."

I'd forgotten all about the new housekeeper.

Six

"It's such a gloomy sound," I said, repressing a shiver. I was referring, of course, to the foghorn. Since the morning when the weather had turned, the sound of the foghorn had been with us nearly all the time.

"Is it?" mused Mrs. Morgan. "I don't even notice it."

"That's because you've always lived here."

"And my father before me, and his before him." Mrs. Morgan popped a tray of corn muffins into the oven and wiped her hands on her apron. I was happy to sit with her in the kitchen. It was the cheeriest room in the house on a day like this. The temporary clear patch we'd had on the morning Mrs. Morgan had arrived was the last of the good weather, and it had been gray and blowy ever since.

"We Morgans and Rileys have always lived along this coast," she continued. "Riley was my maiden name, you know, but it's all the same. Most of the folks in Klamath have been here for generations."

"The Hermans?"

"Lord, no, Amy. Professor Herman came here ten years ago. The college draws new people in now and then, like your dad, but for the most part we stay pretty much the same."

"Do you know the Hermans' daughter, Miranda?"

Mrs. Morgan snorted. "Her," she said succinctly. "Of course I do."

I was pleased at her disapproving tone and wanted to pry a little, but you couldn't go too fast with Mrs. Morgan. She'd tell you so much and no more, and if you tried to go further, her lips would thin out in a determined line and she'd hum a little tune and pretend to be busy with something.

I liked Mrs. Morgan, but my first impression hadn't left me; I still thought she was not a happy woman. She was so tired and worn-looking, and much younger than you'd imagine to look at her, because she'd told me she had a fifteen-year-old daughter. I decided it was because she was a widow and had to work so hard to support her family that she seemed permanently exhausted.

"Do you think this weather will last much longer?" I said, changing the subject.

"Hard to tell. Weather's fickle here. It can be beautiful for days on end and then"—she made a chopping motion with her hand—"Boom! No more sun and a chill like November in the middle of summer." She stared out the kitchen window. "My guess is this'll lift in two or three days, but it'll get worse before it gets better." As if to agree with this gloomy prophecy, the cry of a gull came shrieking down the chimney. I no longer jumped out of my skin at the unearthly sound, but I'd told Mrs. Morgan how it had affected me when I'd first heard it. She laughed now, and sent me a sympathetic look. "Poor Amy," she said. "It takes time to get used to living here, you know. Crozier's Cottage has quite a past."

I held my breath for fear she'd leave it at that, but she seemed to be in a talking mood, even if she had clammed up about Miranda Herman.

"Jacob Crozier built this cottage for his bride," she said, coming to sit beside me at the table. "That was around the turn of the century. By all accounts they lived very happily, until Jacob went off to fight in the First World War. He died over in France, killed in the trenches, they say. His widow was heartbroken. She had loved it here, but without him it got to be too lonely. You can imagine, can't you?" I could imagine all too well.

"She went off to San Francisco with her children. Her oldest son, Jacob, Jr., came back to live here when he was of age. Brought his new wife. That started out happy enough, too, but the girl — she was a city type, a native San Franciscan — hated the solitude after the honeymoon was over. It got to working on her, and folks whispered that she took to drinking. One night she was meandering along the edge of the bluffs. It was midsummer, and not dark yet, and whether or not she'd been drinking I couldn't say, but she fell over the edge. Died of her injuries."

"How horrible," I said. "It seems odd, though. The bluff isn't sheer. She would have to have fallen directly on to the rocks."

"In those days it was sheer. Jacob, Jr., had the

cliff graded and built those little steps down to the cove. He did it for safety's sake and so he wouldn't have to be reminded every time he looked. He married again some years later, but that ended badly, too. In 1960, I remember it well, he drowned out there." She pointed vaguely out the window.

"In the *cove?*" I felt betrayed. "The cove is safe, isn't it? I swim there all the time."

"But he didn't drown in the cove," Mrs. Morgan said. "He swam far out. What he was doing beyond the safe point, nobody ever knew." There was a gloomy silence as we both sat pondering the bad luck of the Crozier family.

"What then?" I asked, not sure I really wanted to know.

"The cottage stood empty for ten years. It had a sort of reputation for being jinxed, and nobody wanted to live here. After a while, though, rumors die out. People forget. Since then, the place has been rented out to visiting professors at the college, or to couples on vacation for the summer. There was a young couple from Sacramento, rented it for the summer in '74, but they only stayed four weeks. Seems they had an accident on the cliff road up the coast. Nobody was hurt, but if the car had skidded ten more feet they'd have gone over the edge. The truth is — none of them stayed very long."

The kitchen, which had seemed so cheery half an hour earlier, suddenly pressed in on me with all its sad secrets. This house had been the scene of so much misfortune it couldn't help but give off an aura of gloom. My first impression had been right, after all. It was impossible to be happy here. I thought of the odd, recurring sensation I had of being watched, and felt a tingling of fear begin at the base of my spine and radiate upward.

"I don't believe in haunted houses," I said defensively.

"Neither do I," said Mrs. Morgan. The silence grew between us until the ticking of the kitchen clock sounded unnaturally loud. Perhaps Mrs. Morgan realized she'd said more than she meant to, for she seemed to be struggling with herself. At last she said: "I do believe there are places that are unlucky, though. They don't start out that way, but if too many tragedies occur in one place . . ." Her voice trailed off, and she gave me a quick look. "Don't listen to me," she said disgustedly. "Amy, you and your father are going to have a fine time here! Don't pay any attention to me. It's this terrible weather. Gets on my nerves."

Since she'd just said she never even noticed the forghorn I knew this wasn't true, but I also knew she hadn't meant to be such a downer. Something was making her unhappy, and whatever it was it had nothing to do with the weather.

"Tell you what," she said, sitting beside me again and taking my hand in her own rough one. "It's a challenge. You and your Dad are going to turn the luck of Crozier's Cottage around!"

I smiled weakly. "Sure," I said. Then I went up to my room to write a letter to my sister. This was always a tricky proposition, because I wanted to be truthful and at the same time avoid sounding negative. While visions of sad ladies falling over cliffs and Jacob, Jr., swimming far out to a watery death danced through my head, I tried to compose a reassuring, cheerful letter for Anne.

I told her about my preliminary sketches, making them sound better than they were, and I embroidered my meeting with Miranda Herman so that Miranda came out sounding wonderful. I'd already described the beauty of the cove, and I was just racking my brain for something fresh to say when I got a sudden image so vivid it nearly made me gasp. I saw Anne, sitting on the sun porch of the house in New Jersey, reading my letter. It was hot, and the trees surrounding the little porch so leafy and green they turned it into a secret bower. Anne's blond hair would fall over one cheek as she chuckled at my description of — what? The gale blowing in, driving clouds of fog swirling against my window? The gulls screaming and the sea lashing against the rocks? What I'd felt was pure homesickness, and what I saw from my window only made it worse. Through occasional rifts in the fog I saw the huge swells rolling in far up the coast, curling into mountainous waves before they hurled themselves with savage force against the black rocks at the foot of the cliffs.

"Mrs. Morgan tells me that the ocean bed beneath the cliffs is a ships' graveyard," I wrote. If I couldn't be cheerful, at least I'd give Anne a sense of the history of the place.

In the nineteenth century, and for hundreds of years before that, ships went astray in the fog and were dashed to bits against those cliffs. The story that haunted me most was one Mrs. Morgan had told me earlier.

"It was a sailing ship, a three-masted schooner," she'd said. "The fog blew in so fast they hadn't any time to get their bearings, and the current pulled them onto the rocks. The ship was dashed against the cliff face, but most of the crew scrambled up onto the ledges and held on for dear life. Some of them were killed by the impact, but a dozen or more managed to cling to those rocks for hours. The sea got rougher as the night wore on, and one by one the sailors were washed off and sucked into the water and drowned. When morning came, there was only one man left. It seemed a kind of miracle to him that he was saved, but it was a mixed blessing. For the rest of his life he had nightmares about that horrible night. He never understood why he was the only one, of all his mates, chosen to survive."

That man had been Mrs. Morgan's great-grandfather.

When I finished the letter I sealed it and got a stamp from my father's study. I asked Mrs. Morgan if she'd mail it for me in Klamath, and she put it in her old leather bag and went to get her oilskin raincoat from the peg in the pantry. Someone came for her regularly in a battered pickup, but in the fog and gloom I could never see who it was. She stood at the door, tying a rain bonnet over her head, and regarded me with tired, kind eyes.

"Remember what I said, Amy. You're going to turn the luck of this place around." Then she opened the door and trudged up the path toward the dim shape of the pickup truck. The bright yellow of her slicker glowed bravely through the mist, and then she was swallowed up.

That night the wind howled around the corners of the house so loudly that even the sound of the foghorn was muted by it. I lay in bed trying to summon my imaginary friend, but for some reason he wouldn't come. In his place I saw a sailor clinging to a rocky ledge while, one by one, his comrades were sucked down to their deaths beneath the cold, gray sea. Down to the ships' graveyard.

Seven

Two days later, the storm blew back out to sea and the sun returned as quickly as it had gone. The sky was even bluer than before, as if it had been washed extra-clean, and I couldn't help but feel better. My father went up to North Point for the day, driving with Professor Herman and leaving me the car. I washed my hair and brushed it until it glowed nearly blue-black, and dressed casually in jeans and a bright red shirt. I had decided to go into Klamath and apply for a card at the library.

"You're new around here, aren't you?" the librarian asked. She watched with interest while I filled out my temporary card, and when I wrote "Crozier's Cottage" as my address she said: "I thought so! You're Professor Hollis's daughter. My cousin, Maudie Morgan, works for your father."

She was a middle-aged woman, and her tone was friendly, but what she said embarrassed me. She made it sound as if Mrs. Morgan was a servant or something, and a girl about my age who had been browsing through the mysteries looked up at her words. She stared at me with that blank look I was becoming accustomed to, and then turned her back.

I checked out three books with my temporary card, barely stopping to see what they were, and fled. The library was up on a hill near the school, and as I walked to the car I saw a blue Mustang convertible zoom up from the main street. There were two couples inside, and I recognized the golden mane of Miranda Herman even from this distance. She was driving, and in the passenger seat beside her sat a big, blond boy I knew had to be Chip Lawson. They were all laughing and carrying on, gunning the motor and hogging the road. As they drew up near me, Miranda slowed the car and went past at a snail's pace. Four pairs of eyes regarded me curiously, and then Miranda called hello. I called back, thinking maybe I'd misjudged her. It seemed she was about to stop the car and introduce me to the others, but she just idled there for a while, smiling. Chip said something to her in a low voice and she slapped his hand and her smile grew wider. She was wearing a bikini top and jeans, and I figured they were all on their way to the lake. I was beginning to feel uncomfortable at the silent treatment and Miranda's cat-that-swallowed-the-cream grin, and then Chip turned the volume up on the eight-track and they roared off. They were all four laughing now, not even attempting to conceal their contempt for me.

I got into the car and clutched the wheel. My hands were shaking with rage and humiliation. What gave them the right to treat me like that?

I'd never done anything to them. When I was calm enough to drive, I went straight through the main street of Klamath without looking left or right and drove back to Crozier's Cottage in record time. The bright sun and blue skies had lost all their charm for me. I braked viciously in the drive and flung myself out of the car without bothering to take my books. I ran down the steps in the side of the bluff and plunked myself down on the sand. Staring out at the water had a calming effect on me, but instead of seething with anger I now found myself staring through a screen of tears. Everything blurred for a while, and then I ordered myself to stop, to gulp back those tears. It would give Miranda Herman so much satisfaction to think that I was blubbering on the beach because of her cold-shoulder treatment! I imagined the look in those superior green eyes if she could see me now, and gradually the anger and hurt and tension drained away and left me feeling curiously empty.

How long I sat like that I don't know, and I could never pinpoint the exact moment I knew I wasn't alone. It happened gradually. People say they can feel eyes boring into their backs, but it wasn't like that at all. I felt no cold chills on the back of my neck, no tingles up my spine — just the firm, absolute conviction that someone else was very near by. I turned, shading my eyes, and stared up at the rocks above the cove.

He was standing on a big boulder about ten feet away, hands in the pockets of his jeans, looking down at me. For several moments I thought I must be dreaming, because he simply couldn't be real. Not this tall, straight figure, perched with easy assurance at the edge of the rock! If he was real I was either asleep or I'd lost my mind, because the stranger was, beyond any doubt, my Ideal Boy. I must have stared at him for a long time, because he shifted his sneakered feet uneasily and gave me a tentative smile.

"Hello," he said. "I'm sorry if I'm trespassing on your private property."

Even the voice was *his* voice — deep but soft, and gentle. His black hair was blowing slightly in the sea breeze, and I could see that it was curly and springy, the way I'd imagined it. Even his smile was the one I'd dreamed about. It quirked up on one side more than the other, giving him a cute, lopsided look that kept him from being too handsome to be true.

"You're Amy, aren't you?"

I nodded. Somehow I managed to find the words to ask him to join me on the sand. I realized he was politely waiting for my permission, and once he had it he bounded down over the rocks with the easy grace of a mountain goat.

"I'm Daniel Morgan," he said, holding out his hand. "I came to pick my mother up."

I took his hand, surprised to find it warm and real instead of a dream hand; I think I'd half expected him to vanish when we touched. His eyes were a very deep shade of blue. Behind the dark lashes they had looked almost black.

"You're Mrs. Morgan's son?" I asked stupidly.

"I'm one of them. I have four brothers and sisters."

"That must be nice." Everything that came out of my mouth sounded inane and stiff. I was still too shocked to muster up even the bare essentials of conversation. I had always felt shy and tongue-tied around boys, but with Daniel Morgan I was behaving like a zombie.

"My mother tells me you're an artist," he said, sitting beside me on the sand.

"Not really." I felt myself blushing, but just as I was searching for a way to qualify this bleak contradiction, Daniel pointed up the coast. "Plenty of scenes worth drawing up there," he said. "I know a fantastic place along the cliff tops. I'll show you sometime, if you'd like."

My throat constricted with joy at the prospect of going anywhere with Daniel Morgan, but all I said was: "Sure. Thanks."

"I've just been laid off," he said cheerfully. "I was working at a logging camp up north, but a fresh crew arrived yesterday and I was the first one to go." He spread his hands and shrugged. "Seniority."

I looked at him curiously. He couldn't be more than eighteen, I thought, but he talked like a man who was already earning his living. "Are you a logger?" I asked.

"Temporarily, when there's work. In the fall I have a scholarship to go to North Point."

"That's where my father's going to teach."

"I know. He's the resident celebrity."

I stared out to sea. Was he mocking me? My father was well known in naturalist circles, but he was hardly a celebrity. "He doesn't think of himself that way," I said. I'd meant to sound light, but it sounded cool and kind of snippy.

"I only meant the college is proud to have him," said Daniel Morgan. He seemed to sigh a little, and then he uncoiled his long legs and sprang to his feet. "I'd better be going," he said. "My mother is waiting. I'll see you around."

He bounded back up the rocks, vanishing as quickly as he'd appeared. I'd driven him away. He'd made a special effort to be nice, and I'd reacted like a real clod. It was always the same, but this one time I'd wanted desperately to open up, to relax and talk to him as easily and naturally as he'd talked to me. Instead I'd come off as a stuck-up, moody, snobbish type scarcely better than Miranda Herman. I hoped I'd get a second chance. I told myself he'd be around Crozier's Cottage again, and then I'd shine the way I longed to do, but deep down inside I knew I'd botched it. *You only get one chance to turn dreams into reality,* I told myself. Daniel Morgan would never understand that he had struck me dumb by being everything I'd always fantasized about but never quite believed existed.

That evening my father suggested going into Klamath to eat at the Timber Tavern. He was in especially good spirits. "Too bad we've already seen the only movie in town, squirrel, or we'd make a night of it." As I brushed my hair I thought how typical it was that my first big date in Klamath should be with my father. I slipped into a white Aran sweater and debated over whether to wear pants or a skirt. At last I decided on a denim skirt. I avoided my image in the mirror, not wanting to see what Daniel Morgan had seen that afternoon. I was sure my reflection would show a sullen, withdrawn girl — a girl no one could love.

Right from the start the evening was doomed. No sooner had the waitress at the Timber Tavern brought our salads and a beer for my father than the doors swung open noisily and Miranda and her friends filed in. My father was sitting with his back to the door and didn't notice, but I managed to look right through Miranda. I didn't want to give her another chance to snub me. They took over the biggest booth in back, and all through the dinner I was aware of them. Miranda kept laughing and calling Chip's name, and they played the jukebox constantly. I imagined they had plenty to say about me — a girl who had nothing better to do than hang out with her father. Daddy had just asked for the check when the door opened and Daniel Morgan walked in.

"Over here, Danny," called Miranda. He headed for her booth like a homing pigeon, and my despair was complete. He passed by our table while my father was up at the cash register, and when he saw me his eyes widened with surprise. He halted for a moment and gave me a half-smile. "Hello, Amy," he said.

"Over *here,* Danny!" Miranda's voice was impatient.

I nodded stiffly at Daniel Morgan, and then he was gone.

Later, alone in my room, I must have replayed that scene a dozen times. I tried to read the look in Daniel's eyes and cringed at the memory of my polite, tight little nod. A high crescent moon had risen over the bay and was turning the water in the cove into liquid silver. The sea was calm that night and lapped against the rocks with a soothing, insistent murmur. The whole scene was indescribably beautiful, and I hated it with all my heart.

I wished that I had never seen Klamath Heights or Crozier's Cottage. More than anything, I wished that I had never seen Daniel Morgan.

Eight

June melted into July, the days continuing hot and glorious. Each day seemed pretty much like the next to me. I swam, I sketched, and I did the marketing in Klamath. When a new movie came to the Capitol, Daddy and I would go to see it and have a pizza at the Timber Tavern together afterward. I no longer felt self-conscious about the other kids, because I just didn't care. Meeting Danny Morgan, and blowing my chances with him, had driven everything else from my mind.

Whenever I saw him now, and I tried not to, I kept the contact as brief as possible. He delivered his mother in the pickup and called for her in the evening, and although I tried to be somewhere else when the old blue truck rattled into our drive, I wasn't always successful. I'd given up my fantasies about Danny ever since I'd learned something from his mother.

"Danny's been up north logging again," Mrs. Morgan said one sunny morning as I was preparing to go to the cove. "He'll be back any time now."

"You must be proud of him," I said lamely. I was thinking about the last time I'd seen him. We'd practically collided at the front door, and although I'd tried not to look into those blue eyes, the power they had over me was irresistible. We'd mumbled a polite hello.

"Of course I am," Mrs. Morgan said. "Danny's got his head screwed on right. He'll make something of himself."

"I imagine he was really popular at school." The words just popped out — I couldn't resist prying when the source was so close.

Mrs. Morgan sighed. "Everyone's always liked Danny," she said, "but I'll be glad when he goes off to North Point. They'll appreciate him there. He'll meet some nice young people instead of hanging around with that Klamath crowd."

I pretended to be examining the frayed edge of my beach towel. "You mean like Miranda Herman?" I said casually.

"That girl!" Mrs. Morgan spat out the word "girl" with more hostility than I'd ever heard her use. "She thinks the sun rises and sets on her precious head. Would you believe it took Danny nearly a year to catch on to what *she* was all about?" Mrs. Morgan yanked the vacuum cleaner from its cupboard space and plugged it in with a vengeance. Over the high whining she shouted: "They went steady practically all last year. He was always mooning around after her, neglecting his studies, running over there to take her places whenever she crooked her little finger! It made me sick to see the way she used him."

"Didn't Miranda care for him?" I yelled back, feeling slightly ridiculous.

"That girl only cares for herself. Oh, she was crazy about him for a while, but she's as fickle as they come. She knew he was going off to college, so she hooked up with someone else." Mrs. Morgan switched the vacuum off and put one hand on her hip. "She threw him over for Dr. Lawson's son. He's a big, blond, grinning idiot — just right for her. After all, a doctor's son is a much better catch for Miranda."

I was surprised at the strength of Mrs. Morgan's anger and decided that her pride was hurt. The very thought of Daniel suffering over Miranda Herman was torture to me. There was something else, too. Even if I had glittered like a Christmas tree when Daniel and I first met, it wouldn't have done any good! He liked women to be beautiful and self-assured and just a little bit snippy. Even at my best, there was no way I could ever compete with the likes of Miranda.

I decided to forget about Danny and concentrate on doing some watercolors to send back to Anne. I'd made half a dozen sketches of the cove and several of Crozier's Cottage from different angles. It was time to go up the coast and see if I could capture the grandeur of that stretch of rocky beach. When I'd assembled about fifteen really good sketches I'd choose the best, do them in watercolor, and send the entire package to my sister.

I took the car and drove along the coast road, trying to select the best spot. I wasn't ready for the high cliffs yet; maybe I never would be. There was still something about them that repelled me. Even the view from my bedroom window had the power to make my fingertips turn slightly cold, and when I remembered Mrs. Morgan's stories about the luckless sailors, I felt a little knot in the pit of my stomach. There was something evil about that place, and I had no desire to get any closer.

The spot I chose was secluded and pretty. The bluffs here were about sixty feet high, and as rounded and full as the shoulders of a very plump woman. To the south I could see the little half-moon of white sand which was my special cove, and the way the land humped up, each hillock higher and higher, to the spot where I sat. Beneath me the sea showed green and blue with bands of deeper, inky blue where the ocean bottom shelved off to deep troughs. The grass around me was spiky and dry, gray-green gorse with an occasional purple flower poking up bravely against the flat rocks.

I began to sketch, feeling the sun warm on my head and the fresh sea breeze in my hair. Whatever else had happened to me, one thing was certain — I was alive to the beauty of Klamath Heights now in a way I'd never been at first. My fear was being replaced by a grudging admiration for the wild loveliness all around me. I might be lonely, but at least I hadn't lost the capacity to appreciate beauty.

When I'd worked for a while, I flipped through the sketchbook, taking a break and comparing my earlier drawings with the more recent ones. I came to the self-portrait I'd done at the cove and stared at it, startled. The face looking up at me was undeniably mine, but how unpleasant it seemed! I'd tried to put all my loneliness and despair into that drawing, and I'd succeeded only too well. I didn't even like the person I'd drawn. She seemed full of self-pity.

"It can't be as bad as that, can it?"

The voice was soft, a little amused. I would have known it anywhere in the world. I turned and saw Danny Morgan, hands in his pockets, standing a few feet away in the grass. He was looking at the ghastly self-portrait. His tone of voice had been slightly mocking, but when he shifted his eyes to me they were full of sympathy. I spoke without thinking.

"I don't like her at all."

Danny smiled, his teeth flashing white in his tanned face. "Go easy on her," he said. "She's new around here." He walked toward me, then stopped, teetering on his heels. "I don't want to bother you if you're working," he said. "I saw the car parked by the bend in the road. I thought — "

"I could use some company," I said. It felt as if the words had been dragged out of me, but my voice sounded calm enough.

"May I see your sketches?" Danny sat beside me. The wind blew his dark hair forward and I wanted to smooth it back. Close up he was so handsome in that dark, mysterious way that I felt almost paralyzed with shyness. Wordlessly, I handed the book to him and tried to keep my eyes from him while he turned the pages.

"Some of these are very good," he said. He

grinned again. "In my humble opinion, this one seems special."

He was pointing to my own favorite—a sketch of the cove I'd done after swimming there one afternoon. I felt I'd captured some of the enchanted quality of it. Haltingly, I tried to explain how I'd sketched the cove more from my feelings about it than from reality.

"Maybe that's what makes it so nice," he said. "Your feelings."

I had one of those flashes then, the kind that determine exactly what's going to happen to you from that point on. I could either play it safe, risking nothing, or I could abandon all caution and risk making a fool of myself. I spoke quickly, before I could change my mind.

"I'm sorry I've been such a nerd," I said. "I know I must have seemed like the most conceited, cold, unfriendly person in the world. The truth is, I'm very shy. It's not easy for me to talk to people I don't know very well, and I come across all stiff and . . ." I searched for the right word, blushing furiously.

"Don't give it another thought," said Danny, smiling. "I'm shy, too, but I have different defense mechanisms. Sometimes I talk too much so I won't have to hear what I'm saying."

I was so overwhelmed at this obvious lie—Danny shy? Impossible!—that I started to babble. I told him all about the cold-shoulder treatment I'd had from the kids in Klamath, careful not to mention any names, and confessed my fear that I'd never make any friends in school.

"They're not such a bad lot," Danny said. "I know just how you must feel, though. It's tough being the new recruit in a town where everyone knows everyone else. We're pretty isolated up here, you know. Some of them probably stared at you because they were surprised to see a new face. They didn't mean to make you uncomfortable. Have you actually met any of them?"

"I had dinner at the Hermans' with my father," I said carefully. "I met Miranda."

"Oh, Miranda." Danny's blue eyes darkened slightly. "You don't want to judge everybody in town by Miranda. She's kind of difficult."

"Difficult?"

"Well, to get along with." He looked out to sea and I realized he didn't want to discuss Miranda Herman.

After an awkward little silence I asked him if he wanted to share the cheese and tomato sandwich I'd brought along, and soon we were behaving almost like old friends. Danny told me about his job in the lumber camps, imitating the crusty old foreman in a way that made me laugh helplessly, and I told him about my ridiculous nervousness when we'd first moved in to Crozier's Cottage and how I'd jumped and screamed every time a gull called down the chimney. Just as I was describing my reaction a seabird flew over and screeched down at us, and we both collapsed with laughter.

I felt so at home with him, and so utterly, ridiculously happy, that it was a shock when he pointed out the position of the sun. It was late afternoon, and time for him to pick his mother up.

"Come on," he said, jumping to his feet and holding his hand out, "I'll follow you back."

I put my hand in his and leaped to my feet as lightly as possible, but the little electric jolt I felt when his warm fingers curled around mine nearly made me lose my balance. I looked down at the ground to conceal my flustered state, and then I felt his other hand slowly smoothing my hair back, forcing me to meet his gaze.

"I've enjoyed this afternoon, Amy."

"Me, too."

"I'd like to see you again sometime."

My heart stood still at the "sometime." No matter how much my defenses had dropped, I was nowhere near confident enough to suggest a time or place. I merely nodded.

"I could show you my favorite place," Danny said softly. "I think you'd like it."

"Yes," I whispered, remembering his earlier offer and my cold response. "I'm sure I would."

He continued to stand like that, his hand warm on my cheek. An odd expression flickered in his blue eyes, and then the moment was gone. We walked back to where my car and his truck were parked, and just before I got in he put his hand lightly on my shoulder.

"I'm glad you let me get to know you, Amy. I was beginning to think you never would."

Those words echoed in my mind all the way home. I could see him, following me, in the rearview mirror, and I had a hard time paying attention to the road. My heart felt full to bursting, and I tried to keep a big, goony smile of bliss from blossoming across my face.

It was the happiest day I had known since coming to California, and it was only the beginning. That's what I kept telling myself: *It's only the beginning.* I couldn't know then that it was the beginning of many things, and that some of them would prove to be more than I'd bargained for.

Nine

The next few weeks passed in a blur of happiness for me. Daniel and I didn't exactly have dates, not at first. We spent time together in a way that felt perfectly natural. In the days following our meeting on the bluffs, we swam in the cove and walked up the rocky shore together, just enjoying each other's company. It was so much like my fantasy. In my lonely moments I had dreamed of just such a relationship; Danny really did bring out the hidden person in me, the girl who could talk easily and unselfconsciously without guarding every word.

We also knew how to be quiet together. In the past I had always felt uncomfortable whenever there was a silence in conversation. I didn't know how to fill it, and as each agonizing second ticked by I had been sure I'd drop straight through the ground with embarrassment. With Danny I knew quiet times that were special, magical. Sometimes there was no need to talk. We would walk side by side, the waves curling at our toes, the sun on our shoulders, and feel no need for words.

"I like the Morgan boy," my father said one evening when Danny had driven off with his mother. "He knows where he's going and he's at peace with himself."

"He's wonderful," I said. "He's not like other boys."

My father gave me an odd look, then smiled. "I know you think the world of him, squirrel, and I'm glad you've found a friend. I just don't want you to get too attached to him. He's going to college next year, and he's bound to make new friends there."

I bit my lip, not knowing what to say. I was all too aware that Danny would move into a new world in the fall, but I didn't want to think that far ahead. I was too happy in the present.

"All I'm saying, Amy, is that you should meet other people your age. You should have lots of friends, not just one." He cleared his throat and I saw that he was slightly embarrassed. "I don't want you to get hurt," he continued. "You've always been a very private person, very intense. Don't stake your whole happiness on one young man, no matter how special he may be."

Poor Daddy! In his funny way he was warning me not to get too involved. He'd never had to talk to me this way before, because I'd never had a real boyfriend. I wondered if it would surprise him to know that Danny had never even kissed me. It was the only cloud in my happy existence. I knew he cared for me, because I could feel it. When he took my hand as we ran into the water or smiled his special, lazy smile into my eyes I felt my knees get trembly and weak. More than anything, I wanted him to put his arms around me and tell me he cared about me. It had to happen soon, and I would wait for however long it took, but in the meantime I had to reassure my father.

"Don't worry, Dad. You can trust me. As a matter of fact, I wanted to ask you if it would be all right to go to the lake tomorrow. Danny wants to take me there so I can meet some of the other Klamath kids."

My father's face brightened. "Splendid," he said. "Just be back in time for dinner. Danny's welcome to join us."

As I was getting ready for bed, I thought about asking Danny to dinner. The fact that his mother was our housekeeper made things tricky. Mrs. Morgan hadn't said anything about us, not to me, anyway, but she didn't seem to disapprove. Probably she thought he was being nice to the lonely professor's daughter just for something to do during the long summer. What would she say if she knew that we were in love? I knew so much about Danny in some ways, and so little in others. He had told me about his love for the wild, unpredictable coast that had frightened me so much at first. He had described what it was like to be a native here and feel the cliffs and the sea in your bones and blood. I knew how he had struggled to maintain top grades while he was playing football for Klamath High, and I knew that he was planning to become a marine biologist.

On the other hand, I knew almost nothing of his life at home. When he disappeared, taking Mrs.

Morgan off in the pickup, it seemed he dropped into a void. He didn't seem to want to talk about it, either. Once, when I ventured to ask him how old he had been when his father died, a shadow passed over his face and he tightened his lips.

"It was a long time ago," he had said.

Daniel Morgan wasn't the sort of person who would be ashamed of his family because his mother worked in other people's houses, so I was forced to conclude that he kept silent about them because there was something painful in his past. Whatever it was, I felt sure it was the reason for Mrs. Morgan's hidden unhappiness, too.

The next day all thoughts of family secrets had vanished. All I could think of was the fact that I'd soon see Daniel. We'd swim together in that blue jewel of a lake I'd only glimpsed from the car. Certainly his taking me there proved something! He would never appear at the gathering place of the Klamath crowd with me by his side if he didn't think of me as someone special. The fear I'd normally feel at the prospect of meeting so many new people was pushed far into the background of my mind. With Danny beside me I didn't need to be afraid of anything or anyone. Not even snide Miranda Herman could make me feel insignificant.

He rattled into the drive on the dot of noon, and I leaped into the seat next to him, eager to be off. He gave me that sideways smile, the one that gave me a catch in my throat, and we spun around in the drive and drove off without saying anything. About halfway into town he announced that the movie at the Capitol was changing at the end of the week. "Would you like to go Friday?"

I nodded, trying to seem casual.

"I thought I'd better stake my claim right now," said Danny. "After today the lines from Klamath to Crozier's Cottage will be buzzing day and night." He said it in a teasing way, but I felt the familiar, weak-kneed tremor all the same. It was the first time he'd ever hinted at wanting me all to himself.

We parked in a small lot next to the sandy beach. There were about a dozen kids lying on striped blankets and splashing around in the cobalt water. On a raft far out I could see a smaller group lounging around, drinking Pepsi from cans. One muscular boy was practicing fancy dives, and every time he missed and belly-flopped a sarcastic cheer came up from the shore.

As we approached the group on the sand I recognized several familiar faces. The girl in the green tanksuit was the one who'd regarded me curiously in the library, and two of the boys lying near her I'd seen from the windows of the supermarket. A brown body turned slowly, propping itself on an elbow, and I recognized the cashier who had looked away from me that first day. It must be her day off.

Don't panic, I told myself. *Danny's here. You're not a stranger now.*

All of them grinned and greeted Danny with joy.

"Where have you been keeping yourself, Danny boy?" asked the cashier.

"Isn't it obvious?" said one of the guys with a wink in my direction. "Hi, I'm Jerry Bell."

Then Danny was introducing me to all of them, and we were spreading our blanket out and settling in as if it were the most natural thing in the world.

"I saw you in the library," said the girl called

Lisa. "The librarian was hassling you. She's okay, but nosy, you know? She doesn't see that many new faces." Lisa smiled, her brown eyes crinkling. "Anyway, welcome to Klamath, pine-tree capital of Northern California."

"Velcome to Klamath, my lovely," said Jerry Bell in a Dracula voice. "Ve need new blood."

"Don't mind him," said Lisa. "He dived into a submerged log last week and hasn't been the same since."

Jerry snapped Lisa with a towel and Joanne Higgins, a silvery blond girl so slender she seemed like something from a fashion magazine, rolled her eyes.

"It's life in the fast lane here, all the way," she deadpanned. "Hope you can stand the pace, Amy."

I had to laugh. Were these friendly, funny, natural people the same hostile, staring figures I'd resented so bitterly in my first weeks here? Either I had been so uptight and withdrawn I'd invested them with a coldness they didn't possess, or they were behaving differently because I'd appeared at the lake with Daniel Morgan.

Danny had already stripped to his suit. His long, brown frame was stretched on our towel and he looked up at me, his blue eyes smiling. He was waiting for something, and I realized that I was still standing in my jeans and shirt. Feeling self-conscious, I pulled my clothes off and stood in my red bathing suit — the only person on the beach without a deep tan. My skin had turned honey-colored from the time spent at the cove, but I was still pale compared to the Klamath set. Joanne and Lisa, with their blond hair and mahogany tans, looked unbelievably striking.

Quickly, I stretched out beside Danny and luxuriated in the warmth of being near him. I was very aware of his bare leg, just inches from mine, and his nearness, combined with the easy, friendly talk and the beauty of the day, made me feel almost reckless.

"Come on," he whispered, when we'd been on the beach nearly half an hour, "let's go in."

The water was spring-fed and cold, but delicious. We swam out twenty feet or so, and then turned on our backs, holding hands, and floated.

"Happy?" Danny squeezed my hand.

"Yes," I said. "They all seem so nice. Especially Joanne."

"I don't like to say 'I told you so,' but" — Danny rolled over and ducked me, laughing as I came up spluttering and indignant — "I told you so."

The day would have been perfect except for one small incident. I suggested we swim out to the raft so I could practice diving. The cluster of kids were still too far away for me to make out specific shapes, but Danny squinted in their direction and shook his head. "Some other time," he said.

Later, when we were sharing sandwiches and drinking Cokes with the others on shore, the raft group came swimming in, sleek as a school of dolphins. As they came closer I saw that Miranda and Chip Lawson were with them. Miranda rose up from the water like some goddess in a painting, except that she was wearing a very modern and very scanty bikini. A silence fell over our group as the others padded across the sand toward us. They were laughing and talking among themselves, but just as they passed our towel Miranda called out to Danny.

Her voice was honey-sweet, but I could detect a sarcastic undertone. I looked up and saw her standing a few feet away, her curvy, tanned body glistening with drops of water and barely concealed by the hot-pink bikini. Danny said hello in pleasant, neutral tones, and Miranda's sly, green gaze switched to me.

"If it isn't Amy Hollis," she said in a surprised voice. "Well, well — it doesn't take you long, does it?" She gave one of her mean little silvery laughs and walked off, swaying her hips. I saw Danny's eyes follow her, and although his expression was unreadable my heart sank. He had recognized that screaming pink bikini from a great distance, and that was why he hadn't wanted to swim to the raft. He wasn't over Miranda Herman yet. Maybe he never would be.

"There she goes, the sweetheart of Klamath High," said Joanne in acid tones. "Don't mind her, Amy. She has a heart of pure ice."

"Danny knows," said Jerry. "He can warn you about the beauteous Miranda." Lisa kicked him, a small, warning kick I wasn't supposed to see.

"Oh, give it a rest," said Danny. "I have better things to think about." He smiled at me as he said it, but Miranda, with her usual instinct for the jugular, had managed to put a dent in my happiness.

It wasn't until we were driving home that I remembered to ask Danny if he'd have dinner with us. His face clouded over a little, and he turned to me. "I'd really like that," he said, "but I can't. Not tonight. There's something I have to do."

I guess my disappointment showed in my face, because he stopped the truck and we sat in silence for a moment. Then he brought his hand up and cupped my cheek so gently it felt like the touch of a butterfly's wing. "Ask me again, will you, Amy?"

I nodded, breathless with the conviction that he would kiss me at last. His face was so close I could feel his warm, sweet breath on my cheek. He seemed to bend even closer, but then the strange, sad look I'd seen before flickered in the depths of his eyes, and he moved away. We drove back without another word to Crozier's Cottage.

"Tomorrow?" he said as I fumbled with the door handle.

"Tomorrow," I agreed.

All that evening I thought about the "something" Danny had to do that night. It was a perfect night, with a high, three-quarter moon riding over the water of the bay and turning the shore silver.

Ten

I didn't really become Danny's girl until the day he finally took me to his special place on the cliffs. Before that we did all the things Klamath couples did when they were going together. We swam at the lake, ate pizza at the Timber Tavern, and went to the movie at the Capitol whenever it changed. We were even recognized as a couple. Lisa didn't say: "Is Danny going to the lake tomorrow?" It was: "Are Danny and Amy going?"

My father gladly gave his permission for me to see as much of Danny as I liked. He trusted Danny and was convinced that most of our dates were spent more in public than in private. He was certainly right about that. It may have pleased *him,* but it was beginning to make *me* feel desperate. I longed to be alone with Danny, the way we had been in the beginning. I wanted him to reassure me that the time we spent together was more than just a way to spend the summer before he went off to college. Miranda Herman had gone off to visit her sister in San Francisco, so I wasn't worried about bumping into her when I was with Danny.

One night, at the Timber, I turned to Joanne and asked her the question that had been tormenting me before I could have second thoughts.

"Did Danny care a lot about Miranda?"

Joanne's dark eyes widened at the unexpectedness of the question, and then she began to pleat the napkin under her Coke very carefully.

"I think he was blinded by her," she said at last. "Miranda can be pretty overpowering, in case you hadn't noticed. I don't think he was in love with her, if that's what you mean."

"He must have been unhappy when she broke up with him, though," I pursued. I felt like the person who keeps prodding a hurt place to see how the pain feels.

"Who told you Miranda broke up with Danny?" Joanne laughed. "It was the other way around," she said. "That's why Miranda gives him such a hard time. It was Danny who left *her*."

Just then Rick, Joanne's boyfriend, asked if Danny and I were going to go with them to a fair down the coast the next day.

"I'm sorry," I said. "We have other plans."

Rick lifted an eyebrow and leered. "They vant to be alone!" called Jerry from across the table.

"We're going to a place where I can do some sketching," I explained.

The truth was more exciting. I was at last going to spend time with him alone, away from these new friends who, no matter how much I liked them, kept us apart. It seemed ironic to me that the very spot I'd found so frightening, so savage, would be the place Daniel loved more than any other.

"I first came here when I was a little boy," Danny told me the next day as we parked the truck in the gorse by the road.

We'd ridden up the spiraling coast road for twenty minutes to reach this spot. It wasn't so far in actual miles, but the going was tricky. The road was pitted with gullies and holes and the curves were hairpin sharp. "I made up my mind then and there. I decided I'd come here at least once a week, no matter how hard it was to get away. It makes me feel" — he flushed a little — "I don't know. Special. Quiet. I've made some major decisions here."

His tone was self-mocking, but I could see he meant it. He took my hand and led me toward the rolling expanse of gray-green scrub; in his other hand he carried the large wicker basket I'd packed our picnic in. I knew we were near the sea, because the road hugged the coastline all the way up, but all I could see was the endless field of gorse. There was a sort of beaten path through the scrubby green, and we set off through it.

It was another blue and gold day, and the fresh breeze sweeping up from the Pacific made your heart sing. Far out over the horizon I could see gulls wheeling, and soon I could smell the sea. It was there, just over the next rise, or the next. We trudged along over the flat, bleak terrain and I remembered what I'd felt when my father first brought me to Klamath Heights. It had seemed that we might drive straight over the edge of the world.

"Close your eyes," said Danny. He led me on a few more paces. "Trust me," he said. When I opened my eyes the entire Pacific was spread out before me. It seemed to fill the whole horizon, blending into the sky in a blanket of blue that covered the earth. We were very high, so high I felt almost as if I were in an airplane. I shook my head as if to clear it and held Danny's hand hard.

"Where are we?"

"Just above the cliff that juts out at the point. See? There's the lighthouse."

So far below it looked no bigger than a pale rock was the white tower. Danny led me along a small path that ran parallel to the sea, but I dug my heels into the ground. "Can't we stay here? Where are we going?"

He pointed, and I saw that the small path narrowed to a kind of single-file cart track before it plunged down and lost itself in a huge, flat gray rock. "Please, Danny. I don't want to go there. It looks dangerous."

"Trust me," he repeated. "It's not dangerous so long as you're with me. I know every inch of this place. You're perfectly safe."

It wasn't so bad at first. There was plenty of space between us and the edge of the cliff. I could feel the drop, actually *sense* it, but I couldn't see it. I followed along after him, putting my feet where his had been and clutching his hand. Just when I was beginning to feel foolish for my earlier fears, we reached a point where the ground fell sharply away on the seaward side. I made the mistake of looking down and nearly screamed.

It was like looking into a blue abyss. The sea was so far beneath us I grew dizzy with fear. I had a sudden image of a tightrope walker I'd seen in a circus once. My impulse was to close my eyes, just as I'd done then, but this time I was the one on the high wire, and there was no net to catch me if I fell.

"Don't look," Danny commanded. "It looks more dangerous than it is. You're safe, Amy. I wouldn't let anything hurt you."

It was those words that gave me the courage to go on. Later, Danny showed me how my fingernails had carved little half-circles in his palm, but at the time I was aware only of putting one foot in front of the other and praying that the beating of my heart wouldn't knock me over into that blue cavern. The narrow path at the rim of the cliff was only about fifteen feet long, but for me it might as well have been fifteen miles. I leaned as far away from the seaward side as possible, and I didn't make the mistake of looking down again. I was aware of an odd sound which seemed to come from the rocks ahead of us, but I was too concerned with getting to that flat, safe-looking expanse to think much about it.

"Here we are," said Danny, bringing me safely to the flat ledge. "You can relax now."

We were on a huge, smooth ledge that was as flat and level as a table, and I breathed a sigh of relief. The sound was much more noticeable now. Danny led me across the rock toward it, firmly holding my hand in his and smiling at my hesitant steps. The sound swelled all around us now, musical and strange, like a symphony where all the lower notes have been taken away. It sounded like the voice of the sea itself, and just before we came to the edge I realized that it was the voices of tens of thousands of seabirds. Occasionally I could hear one gull screaming over the general sound, but then the note would be lost in the huge, swelling chorus.

We stopped a few feet from the edge, and Danny pointed silently. All around us, in the ledges of the cliffs, were crannies and holes, and in each one whole families of birds nested. Far down I could see gulls and terns wheeling below us, and even further down, the sea boiled and crashed against the black rocks. It made me queasy to look down at the sea, but I was fascinated by the birds.

"It's like a high-rise apartment building," I whispered. "An apartment building for seabirds."

"And we're in the penthouse," said Danny, laughing at my imagery.

"They sound almost human."

"I've always thought they sounded like mermaids," said Danny. "Remember the siren song that drove sailors onto the rocks?"

I shivered, imagining it all too vividly. This was the very place where Danny's great-great-grandfather had been shipwrecked. In one of those cavernous ledges hundreds of feet down, he and his mates had clung for safety during the long, terrifying night. Below us was the ships' graveyard.

"Are you cold?" Danny slipped his arm around my shoulders, and I shook my head. This place had an awesome beauty in spite of the aura of danger, and I could understand why he loved it. He spread his denim jacket on the rock and placed our wicker basket near by. I was about to sit down when I realized that my legs were trembling oddly. I had been even more afraid during the dangerous part of the walk than I'd admitted.

"Amy." His voice was soft, almost a whisper. "You're safe with me, you know. I told you, I'd never let anything hurt you."

His arms came around me then, and we sank down to our knees. I could hardly breathe. My heart was knocking painfully against my ribs again, but this time it wasn't fear that made me tremble. It was something else. I could feel his strong hands on my back, and then he bent and kissed me gently. His lips were so warm, and tender, that I almost felt I might cry.

It was my first kiss, and it was everything I had ever dreamed of and more. I felt my arms go around him, and then I was kissing him back, and all around us the siren song of the birds filled the air. I understood something, then. Daniel hadn't kissed me until now because his feelings were as strong as my own. He had wanted to wait until he was sure I was ready.

When we broke apart we were both trembling. Danny just cradled me in his arms for a while, and then we smiled into each other's eyes, making a sort of pledge without words.

That was the happiest afternoon of my life, I think. We sat together quietly, just content to be with each other. When we ate our picnic lunch of cheese sandwiches and hard-boiled eggs we demolished every scrap, yet I don't think either of us tasted anything. I don't even remember what we talked about, because words suddenly seemed unimportant. The time passed so quickly that I was amazed when Danny pointed out the sun, riding low in the sky.

"I'll never forget this day," I told him when we were preparing to leave our rock.

"I don't want you to, Amy."

I wasn't as frightened on the way back, even though the dizzying drop appeared even more sheer from the ledge. I still couldn't look down, though. I doubted that I'd ever want to.

When we got back to the truck I noticed something strange. Where we had been, a soft blanket of sea mist swirled and eddied in the late afternoon light. Even as I watched, it grew thicker, obscuring the path.

"Look," I breathed. "It's all covered up."

Danny kissed the tip of my nose. "That's why we had to leave. So long as it's clear, I know we're safe, but it gets misty suddenly. In a real fog, it would be dangerous." He put his arms around me and held me close for a moment. "Promise me one thing," he said. "Promise me you'll never come here without me."

"I'd never want to."

"I mean it, Amy. I know every rock, every turn in the path. I know this place like the palm of my hand, but you don't. Part of the cliff is badly eroded. Someone who didn't know might decide to walk there." He pointed to a deceptively safe-looking shoulder of green. "And do you know what would happen?"

I shook my head, feeling the earlier fear return.

"It would crumble away under them. There's no support from beneath. That's why I want you to promise me. *Don't ever walk alone here, Amy.*"

I thought of the horror of it — the ground giving

way, the long, sickening fall through space, the sea hurtling closer until you landed, broken, on the rocks beneath. "I promise," I said.

"That's my girl," Danny said, and the horror faded.

Eleven

Miranda came back in time for the Labor Day picnic, just before school started. It was Joanne who told me, calling me at Crozier's Cottage the day before the big event.

"I just wanted you to know she's back," said Joanne in a hesistant voice. "I hate people who pry in other's business, Amy, but you're new here and I wanted you to be warned."

"Warned? You make it seem as if Miranda is after me!" I laughed, but I felt uneasy.

"The picnic is a big tradition here. Everybody goes — all the kids from school and the ones who're going off to college. It lasts all day and as late as our parents will let it. It's your typical 'Farewell to Summer' blast."

"What does that have to do with Miranda?"

"When she left for San Francisco, you and Danny were just beginning to date, right? And now you're a real couple. You're Danny's girl, Amy. Miranda is a real sore loser. Of course she's not *after* you, but she'll try to make you look dumb, or embarrass Danny, or . . ." Joanne's voice trailed off.

"Thanks, Jo," I said. "I appreciate the warning."

"Forewarned is forearmed. We're all on your side, Amy. Miranda Herman is a spoiled, spiteful little witch. If Chip weren't so dumb he'd leave her flat, but he's dazzled."

All that afternoon, while I got in Mrs. Morgan's way putting the picnic together, I pondered Joanne's words. Danny, too, had been dazzled by Miranda's beauty, and it still hurt to think about them together. I was frying chicken, torturing myself with images of them together, when Mrs. Morgan startled me.

"Is Daniel taking you to the picnic?" she asked, appearing in the kitchen doorway. I nodded. Mrs. Morgan rarely gave any sign that she was aware of our relationship, yet she clearly knew all about it.

"You might want to put this in your hamper," she said, producing a foil-wrapped package from the depths of her duster pocket. "It's just some cookies I baked — molasses and raisin. They're Daniel's favorite." She nearly blushed, and I would have hugged her if I didn't know it would embarrass her.

"Thank you," I said. "It was really nice of you to go to the trouble."

"No trouble, Amy." Mrs. Morgan took a seat at the kitchen table. "Dan's a big boy now, and I wouldn't presume to tell him what to do. Even if I didn't think you were one of the nicest girls around,

I'd hold my tongue." She gave me one of her rare smiles. "I just want you to understand something. When Danny goes off to college he'll be living at home, same as always, but chances are you won't see quite as much of each other. He's got to work, you know. Between his studies and the part-time jobs, he'll be pretty busy."

Now she was definitely blushing. "I wish we didn't need his help to keep the family going, but we do. I depend on Danny a lot. In some ways he's had to grow up too fast, I suppose, but it couldn't be helped."

"I understand," I said softly. And I did. Danny had already told me he'd be holding down a part-time job at the lumberyard in addition to his studies. I knew he had to help his family, and I admired him for it. I understood something else, too, and it made me glow with pleasure. Mrs. Morgan, like Joanne, was definitely on my side.

All Klamath celebrated Labor Day in a big way. My father was going to a party at the Hermans, and afterwards, when it was dark, they were going to watch the fireworks over the lake.

"I don't have to warn you, do I, *sciurus*?" Daddy said the next day, as I was packing the hamper with cold chicken, pickles, hard-boiled eggs, and the cookies Mrs. Morgan had made.

"Warn me about what?" It seemed I was getting an awful lot of warnings lately.

"I've been told a lot of drinking goes on at the young people's picnic. I don't have to tell you that's out, do I?" I shook my head indignantly. I didn't even like the taste of beer, let alone the hard stuff.

"And driving — there are always a lot of accidents on these roads around holidays. I'm sure Daniel's steady enough; I have complete trust in him. After all, I trust him with my most precious possession, don't I?"

I hugged my father then, feeling his tweedy jacket scratch my cheeks. "I won't get into any car other than Danny's," I assured him.

"Good." He patted my back absentmindedly. "I expect you home no later than eleven," he said. "Ten hours of partying is enough for anyone."

The picnic officially started at one in the afternoon, but when Danny and I parked near the lake shore the sand was already swarming with kids. There were people I'd never seen before, and lots of older guys, some of them nearly twenty by the looks of them. We joined Lisa and Jerry and Joanne and Rick on a blanket near the water's edge.

"Who are all these people?" I asked Joanne.

"The youth of Klamath," she said mock-dramatically, "all preparing to bid farewell to the glory of summer."

Despite her joking tones, I felt momentarily sad. The summer, for me, *had* been glorious. Ever since the day on the cliffs when Danny had first kissed me, I had been so happy it was almost scary. Every day I woke up knowing I was the luckiest girl in California. I never grew tired of being with Danny. Whether we swam in the cove or went up to our special place or hung out with the others in town, I knew a unique joy I'd never experienced before. I felt cherished and special — almost as if I were leading a charmed life.

"Don't be sad," Danny said in a low voice, so the others couldn't hear. It was amazing the way we could read each other's thoughts. "All summers have to end," he said, "but there'll be others." He smiled that lazy, lopsided smile and I felt myself tingle right down to my bare toes.

"Come on, you lovebirds," said Lisa. "This is a party, not a wake! Let's party." She turned the volume up on Jerry's radio and they began to dance. All along the beach, couples were dancing or running into the water with loud rebel yells. I could see Josh Banks, a boy Danny's age, swimming out to the raft with a six-pack of soft drinks held up in one hand. As he sidestroked along he was cheered on by the thirsty group already settled on the raft. It was all good fun, innocent and cheerful, if a little loud. It continued like that all afternoon. We would run in for a dip and come back to collapse on the blanket and nibble away from our hamper. Occasionally someone would remark on the fact that Miranda and Chip were absent, but nobody really seemed to care.

They arrived just when we were lighting the giant bonfire in the area set aside by the Klamath Parks Commission. Danny had gone off to the small concessions stand to get two grape drinks, and I was talking to Joanne when Miranda strolled by, arm-in-arm with Chip. Miranda walked as if she owned the beach and we were all serfs doing her bidding. She waved at friends, giving them her tight, cool little smile, and her green eyes reflected pride in the knowledge that everyone was watching her. There was something about Miranda that drew all eyes to her, and it wasn't just her silvery blond hair and terrific figure. Miranda commanded attention because she *expected* it. I guess you could call it supreme self-confidence, but I'd prefer to call it something else: arrogance. There's something fascinating about a sixteen-and-a-half-year old girl who figures she owns the world — something that makes you stare at her even when you don't want to.

"Look at Jerry and Rick," muttered Joanne. "Miranda's the cobra and they're the mongooses. Or is it mongeese?"

Miranda halted, spun around on one slender, tanned foot, and headed for us. She couldn't possibly have overheard Joanne, but I felt a little lurch of apprehension.

"Amy!" She called to me as if we were the best of friends, smiling so radiantly it was almost blinding. Chip lurked behind, not following her. "How *are* you?" Her voice dripped honey; if you didn't know her you'd think she was being sincere. "How was your summer?"

"Fine," I said. She was standing a couple of feet away, her eyes flickering over me the way they'd done when I first met her.

"I should think so," she said, raising her voice and turning to address half a dozen people. "These Eastern girls," she sighed. "You just can't compete with them, can you? They move in on poor little ol' us, and next thing you know they're amusing themselves with their servant's sons."

I think I gasped at the crudeness of it, but what she said next really took my breath away. "One thing's sure. Danny will certainly pull down straight *A*'s at North Point. Amy's Daddy can't flunk his daughter's boyfriend, can he?"

I became aware that Danny was standing just behind me and had heard every word so cruelly intended for him. He took my hand but said nothing. "Just kidding, of course," said Miranda. She blew him a kiss and sauntered off.

There was an awkward silence, and then Joanne said in indigant tones, "Someday someone will tell Miranda where to get off, and I sure hope I'm there to hear it."

"Just ignore her," said Jerry. "She can't stand to be ignored."

"I'd rather drown her," said Lisa.

Only Danny was silent, pretending the whole thing hadn't happened. We watched the bonfire leap up together, and when it grew dark and a little chilly, he wrapped me in a sweater, hugging me. I wanted to ask him how he could let Miranda talk about him that way, but every time I looked at him he seemed closed-off and remote. Once a slender, pretty girl with dark hair passed by and called hello. Her eyes rested on me briefly and then swerved away. "Who is she?" I asked.

"My sister," said Danny, smiling wryly. "Maggie is a year younger than you. You'll meet her when school starts."

When the fireworks started I leaned back against his shoulder and went "Oooo" and "Ahhhh" along with everyone else, but my heart wasn't in it. Miranda had seen to that; Miranda, and Danny's strange silence about the whole episode. While green and red flowers burst in the sky above us like mammoth shooting stars, I could only think of what Miranda had said, and imagine the cutting, witty remarks I should have offered in reply.

Some of the kids were drinking beer, and a few of the older boys were roaring around on motorbikes on the shore road above, and I remembered what my father had said. When the last Roman candle shot up over our heads, I turned to Danny and said I wanted to go home.

"It's only nine-thirty," he said. "I thought your curfew was eleven tonight."

"I have kind of a headache," I lied. "Must have been all that sun and the fireworks."

Even to my own ears, it sounded like a feeble excuse, but I couldn't tell Danny my real reason. I just couldn't stand to see, in the radiant light from the last trailing shooting star, the expression of spiteful glee in Miranda's gaze. She was sitting directly across from us, and her eyes rarely left Danny's face.

When we arrived at Crozier's Cottage Danny cut the motor and said, eyes straight ahead: "Amy, I'm sorry about what Miranda said. She's an unhappy girl, and you mustn't pay any attention to her. I don't."

"Unhappy?" I felt betrayed. "That isn't the word I'd use. Miranda specializes in making other people feel unhappy, or hadn't you noticed?"

"And what kind of person does that?"

"A vicious, spiteful one." I couldn't seem to stop the words. That Danny should make excuses for

Miranda made me see red. "What does *she* have to be unhappy about, anyway? She has everything anyone could want."

"You're wrong," said Danny in a harsh voice, and then suddenly he was kissing me almost fiercely, with a passion I had never felt from him before. My anger melted away, and I threw my arms around him, digging my fingers into his curly hair and feeling my whole body go strangely weak. It was Danny who broke away. "Amy, Amy," he whispered, "you're worth ten Miranda Hermans. If only you knew."

There were a million questions I wanted to ask him, but just then my father's car turned into the drive and the mood was broken. Daddy looked so young, boyish almost, that I felt a stab of anger at Miranda's jibes. My father wouldn't ever give a student *A*'s because he was my boyfriend — the very idea was ridiculous, and it only showed the way Miranda's shifty mind worked. I said good night to Danny and went straight up to bed, feeling confused and angry.

When I went to sleep I dreamed that Danny and I were at our special place on the cliffs, sitting quietly, holding hands and listening to the sirenlike sound of the birds. At first it was a beautiful dream, and then suddenly, without warning, I was alone on the cliff and the darkness of night was all around me. *Danny!* I cried. *Where are you?* There was no answer, only the screaming of the gulls, and the sea, so far below, pounding with an insistent rhythm on the rocks. I was paralyzed with dread, because I couldn't run back to safety. One false step —

I woke up cold with fear, my teeth chattering. It was a long time before I fell asleep again, and when I awakened in the morning I knew, beyond doubt, that the summer was really over.

Twelve

Klamath High, that gleaming, ultra-modern structure on the hill, was pretty old-fashioned in spirit. For one thing, girls were not allowed to wear jeans. Joanne had told me that most of the girls wore simple skirts and shirts or sweaters, although some got around the no-jeans rule by wearing corduroy pants. I felt right at home in my denim wraparound skirt and blue checked shirt, but back in New Jersey I'd have been considered overdressed.

Another unwelcome feature was alphabetical seating, which was the rule. It meant I'd be seated behind Joanne, but Miranda would be in front of her — Herman, Higgins, Hollis.

"I'd like to welcome our newcomer," said Mrs. McAllister, our homeroom teacher. "Amy Hollis, who lives in Klamath Heights, is an addition to the senior class." Of course, I was the *only* addition. The entire senior class consisted of thirty students, twenty from Klamath and ten from rural areas.

"That's a homey touch," whispered Joanne.

Maggie Morgan, Daniel's younger sister, was in my next class, French. I smiled at her and was about to introduce myself when she turned pointedly away. I studied her haughty little profile and thought how much she looked like Danny. Maggie had the same heavily fringed blue eyes and wild black hair, but unlike Danny she was sullen and elaborately indifferent. At least, I thought she was until some of her friends straggled in to the class. Then her face lit up in a wide grin and I was forced to acknowledge that Maggie Morgan's indifference was reserved for me.

I watched the faces in that French class, and gradually one fact emerged. There were definitely two distinct and separate camps at Klamath High — the rulers and the outsiders. Girls like Maggie Morgan belonged to the latter. Maggie's mother worked for other people, in their houses, and Maggie didn't have the money for expensive blazers or designer jeans.

Danny, of course, had been able to bridge the two camps because he was a football player and popular, but he was an exception to the rule. I belonged nowhere. Maggie would always feel uncomfortable with me because her mother was our housekeeper, and Chip and Miranda and their crowd would ignore me because I was an outsider.

In the cafeteria, at lunchtime, the caste system was even more marked. The kids from farms in the area huddled together at one table, while Maggie and her friends took over another. Chip and Miranda and *their* inner circle were firmly installed at a big round table near the windows. I headed for the table where Joanne and Lisa were sitting. Miranda was staring at me all through lunch. I was glad when the bell rang for the next class.

By the end of the school day I was exhausted. It was the effort of feeling all those new eyes assessing me, more than anything else. I wished with all my heart that Danny could be waiting for me, but he would still be up at North Point, completing his first day of college. I wouldn't see him for several days, but I knew he'd call me that night.

"Want to come to the Timber for a Coke?" asked Joanne, catching up with me on the school steps.

"I'd love to, but I have to get the bus home. My father drops me off in the morning, but he's still up in North Point."

The yellow bus which transported the rural kids was waiting in the drive, and I climbed on, feeling deprived. The bus was already half-filled, and when I headed down the aisle in search of a seat it grew very quiet. All the talk and laughter stopped, and I felt as if I were running the gauntlet. At last I sank into a seat in back, only to be humiliated by the loud voice of the driver.

"Where are you going, Miss? You — in back. You're new, aren't you?"

"Crozier's Cottage, up on the Heights," I replied.

"Crozier's Cottage," repeated the driver. "Well, well."

There were a few snickers, and then the last few passengers got on and the bus groaned into action and went lumbering down through the main street of Klamath. I could see Joanne and Rick disappearing into the Timber Tavern, and I felt wistful. I stared out the window as the bus made the now familiar journey along the twisting road above the coast, and when we came to a stop at the cottage drive I walked to the door of the bus. "Thank you," I called as I swung down the steps.

The house was as silent as a tomb (it wasn't one of Mrs. Morgan's days), and I turned on the radio for company while I changed into jeans and sneakers. They were playing a song that always made me think of Danny, and I reminded myself once more how lucky I really was. I thought of what I'd write to Anne about my first day of school. It's kind of a no-win situation, I'd tell her, but I can handle it. Ever since meeting Danny, I'm a different person. You wouldn't believe how un-negative your sister is these days!

I grabbed an old flannel shirt and went outside. The early fall air was sweet and warm, the sun still bright. I headed for the cove. I thought I'd walk up the beach a little way and write my letter to Anne there, sitting on one of the broad, flat rocks. Armed with note paper, a ballpoint pen, and a russet pear in my bag, I set out.

The ocean seemed to know the summer was over, even if the sun didn't. The water was a deeper, inkier blue, and it looked cold and less friendly. The green bands, which were so noticeable from the cliffs, looked almost black from my vantage point. When I'd selected my rock and propped my note pad on my knees, there was a new problem. It was windier than I'd thought, and the breeze sent my pages turning over as if an invisible hand was reading the blank paper at a superhuman speed. At last I gave up and ate my pear, taking small bites and savoring the tart, juicy flavor as long as I could.

I'm not sure how it was I first noticed the men. They were so far away they appeared like dots on the horizon — little black ants scampering around on the rocks up near the point. They were too distant for me to hear their voices, and they weren't dressed in bright colors, but something alerted me to their presence. It was so unusual to see anything but seabirds on those rocks, I thought I might be mistaken, but as I stared I knew there could be no mistake. The forms were definitely human, and there were two of them.

I knew they couldn't be fishermen because there was no boat, and fishermen didn't haunt the waters beneath the cliffs. But why would anybody else be climbing around on those rocks? There was no way to get there except by sea. You'd have to be a mountain goat to find a way down those cliffs; just imagining it made me dizzy. I wished I'd brought my father's bird-watching binoculars. I even thought of running back for them, but something told me the men would be gone by the time I returned. Even as I watched, one of them disappeared behind a rock, and then the other seemed to melt away before my eyes.

All the way back to the house I puzzled over what they could have been doing there, and by the time I'd reached the front door I'd decided to scan the cliffs with binoculars from my bedroom window. When I let myself in I heard the phone ringing, and cliffs, men, and binoculars vanished from my mind when I picked it up and heard Danny's voice.

Sometimes I wonder what would have happened if I'd mentioned the men to him that day. As it was, I didn't even think about them for another week.

Thirteen

"Why doesn't your sister like me?" I looked into Danny's eyes as I asked the question, because I'd discovered I could read more there, sometimes, than from what he said. This time it didn't seem to work. His face stayed perfectly in control; he didn't even blink.

"What makes you think she doesn't?"

Well, I could have gone on about that for an hour, but I didn't want to bad-mouth Maggie, so I only said: "She kind of avoids me. When I say hello to her she looks away."

"Maggie's strange," said Danny. "She's very smart, but she doesn't warm up to people easily."

"Kind of the way I used to be," I mused, but Danny wasn't about to let that one slip by.

"No. Not like you." And then he put his arm around me and slowly ruffled my hair, and the subject of Maggie was dropped.

We were at a party at Lisa's house, and it was

the first weekend after the beginning of school. Lisa lived in a pretty but modest house near the lake. Her father was one of the chief foremen at the Klamath Lumber Mill, where Daniel would be working part-time, starting the following week. Lisa was a fabulous cook, and she'd made a wonderful buffet supper of lasagne and green salad, crusty bread, and key lime pie for dessert. As I recall, everybody was talking about who'd be elected Harvest Queen.

"Miranda, of course," said Joanne, wrinkling her nose.

The Harvest Queen had to be a senior girl, and she was chosen from a slate of five candidates. Nobody seriously doubted that Miranda would win, even though so many people disliked her. Somehow, she seemed so *right*.

"We have to consolidate," said Jerry. "We all have to get behind Lisa or Joanne. No divisions. Solidarity."

"Why not Amy?" said someone. "We've had a blond queen for three years running. I'm sick of blondes."

That broke everyone up, fortunately, and I was prevented from pointing out that the only people who'd vote for me were right there, in Lisa's living room.

That night, Danny parked the truck on the deserted stretch of road above Crozier's Cottage. "You're so lovely, Amy," he whispered as he took me in his arms. "So lovely." There was a sound of despair in his voice, but before I could wonder why I was caught up in the intensity of his kisses. It seemed almost as if I might melt into him, forever, so that we became one person. Always before, it was Danny who would break away. He would say something funny, or hold me gently, soothingly, until the pounding of our hearts diminished. Tonight the strength of my own feelings frightened me, and it was I who laid my head against his shoulder finally and whispered that I loved him so much I was afraid.

"There's nothing to be afraid of," he murmured against my hair. "I want to be with you always, Amy. I'd never hurt you."

Always. I hugged the word close to me. I knew Danny would never deceive me. I trusted in him absolutely, even if he did get evasive when I asked him questions about his sister.

I decided to ask Joanne instead. During lunch period the following Monday I saw Maggie Morgan laughing at her table in the cafeteria, and she looked so lovely and carefree I felt a stab of pain. How could this girl, who looked so much like Danny, dislike me so much when she didn't even know me? In French class she had shown her hatred openly. Someone had asked her how her mother was, and Maggie had said, quite distinctly, "Ask Professor Herman's daughter. She sees more of her than I do."

When I put the question to Joanne she took a long time to answer. She poked around in her plate of hot-dog casserole, made a face, and sighed. "Maggie's basically very nice," she said at last, "but she carries a chip around on her shoulder. When her father ran off, she was only five, but she adored him.

I think she never got over it. The fact that her mother has to support them — "

I had stopped listening at the crucial sentence.

"What do you mean? I thought Mr. Morgan was dead."

Joanne looked at me levelly. "Is that what Danny told you?"

"He never says anything about it. I just assumed — "

"Danny and Maggie's father disappeared ten years ago. Just left without a word. He's never been back, and he's never sent them so much as a postcard."

I felt my heart constrict with pity. I had felt sorry for the Morgan family before, and now I felt even sorrier. My own mother had died, but I knew she loved us. To have a father who deserted you and didn't even care enough to write — it seemed awful.

"Poor Maggie," I said. "Poor Mrs. Morgan." And, unspoken: *My poor Danny.*

That day, after school, I walked over to the Klamath Lumber Mill. I had to see Danny, even though it meant walking all the way back to Crozier's Cottage. I found him in the lumberyard, loading two-by-fours into a truck. The look on his face when he saw me was one I'll never froget. There are all sorts of ways to be surprised, and some of them aren't too pleasant, but the look on someone's face when the surprise is a nice one is unforgettable. His blue eyes lit up as if a candle had been placed behind them.

"Amy! What are you doing here?"

"I just wanted to say hello," I said. I only

stayed a few minutes, but so much love passed between us I felt as if he'd kissed me. It was worth the long walk home, even though my father got back before I did and chewed me out for not taking the bus.

"I had something important to do," I said. "Something that couldn't wait."

My father tilted his head on one side and studied me closely. "Anything wrong?" he said "Anything you want to tell me?"

"Did you know Mrs. Morgan's husband deserted her ten years ago?"

"No. I guess I didn't think it was any of my business."

"But didn't you tell me she was a widow?"

He furrowed his brow. "Not that I can recall. I think I said she was head of the family. On her own. I'm sorry to hear — " He didn't finish the sentence, and I knew he was thinking about my mother. For the first time I realized just how deep his loss had been, and I ached for him. Not until you truly love someone can you imagine what it would be like to have her die. I looked at my father, standing in the middle of the room in his tweedy jacket and feeling lonely, and I wanted to cry.

"Daddy, there's shrimp salad for dinner tonight. Mrs. Morgan left it in the fridge." Mrs. Morgan's seafood dishes were wonderful, and my father smiled his appreciation. "That's great, squirrel," he said, but the sad look remained in his eyes. All during supper I kept thinking about how Dad should marry again. He was so handsome, and such a decent, gentle man. But for all my wanting him to be happy, the whole idea of his remarrying made me feel uneasy.

I remember that evening as one of the last before things changed. I can see us so clearly, sitting in the dining room, Daddy with his private thoughts and me with mine — two people who loved each other but couldn't always find the words to express it. I remember it partly because, after what happened at the end of that week, I didn't give much thought to my father at all.

I had finished my homework early that Friday afternoon, because Danny and I were going to the movies at night. When I knew I was going to see him I became nervous with anticipation, and it seemed as if the time passed with a torturous slowness. I decided to take my sketchbook and walk along the beach waiting for inspiration. At the last minute I remembered the binoculars, but they weren't in their familiar place in my father's study. He had taken them to the school; probably there was a field trip today.

Even though it was still only September, there was a chill in the air and the salt breeze smelled as tart and snappy as little green apples. The waves seemed to have a different pattern now. I could see them forming from a long distance away in long, smooth combers that reared up into mountainous shapes before crashing against the shore. The sun was setting earlier now, and at four in the afternoon there was a hint of the darkness to come. A long way away, at the point, I could see plumes of sea mist drifting across the cliff face, which was Danny's and my special place. It looked remote and forbidding, and reminded me I should turn back. I'd walked much farther than I'd intended.

I saw the men about a quarter of a mile ahead of me, walking in my direction. There were three of them this time, but I was sure that two of them were the men I'd seen clambering on the rocks, because who else would be on this lonely stretch of beach? In all the time I'd lived at Crozier's Cottage, I had never seen another human being walking here. Instead of turning back, I continued to walk toward them. It was as if something compelled me to get a better look. Even though the sight of those figures coming nearer filled me with an odd sense of fear, I had to see them at close range.

A large outcropping of boulders cut across the sand at one point, obscuring my view, and when I'd reached it I knew they must be very close. What if they were waiting on the other side, waiting for me to walk right into them? I hesitated, judging how far they had come. Surely they should have rounded the boulders and be in view again, yet they seemed to have vanished. The tide was coming in, and the waves reached almost to the boulders' edge. I knew that later, in an hour or two, the water would cover the spot where I stood and it would be impossible to walk to the point. Impossible to get there, except in a boat.

Suddenly, I wanted to run. I wanted to be back at Crozier's Cottage, away from the pounding sea and the darkening, desolate beach. I turned and walked away swiftly almost — but not quite — running. I'd only gone a few yards when I heard a voice calling after me. "Hey! You!"

I turned and saw nothing but the empty stretch of rocks and sand. "You!" called the voice again, and I followed its source to the pile of boulders. The man was standing at the summit, hands on his hips, looking down at me. He was about my father's age, and he was dressed in dark pants and a heavy, dark sweater. A black knit cap was pulled low around his face, and he was smiling as if the sight of me amused him. It was not a pleasant smile. Gradually, I realized that another man was squatting on a ledge of rock just below him. He was younger, and his face was perfectly expressionless although he, too, was watching me carefully. The third member of the group, dressed like the other two, was looking up the coast as if scouting for something. I couldn't see his face at all.

"It's dangerous to walk here," said the first man. "Don't you know that?" He smiled, and the whiteness of his teeth reminded me of a picture I'd stared at as a child. It was of the wolf, in *Little Red Riding Hood,* dressed in the harmless granny's nightcap.

"It's dangerous," he repeated. "Best keep to your own backyard, girlie." Then, as if at a signal, they disappeared back over the rocks and vanished. I stood still there for a moment or two, feeling as if I had come face to face with evil. Then I turned and hurried along back toward home. It seemed important not to run, because I was sure they were watching me. It was only a feeling, but then the feeling became a certainty and I turned to look back once more.

Only one man was silhouetted against the rocks, and he was the one who had been turned away before. The look on his face was different from the others', neither menacing nor blank, but somehow sad. Something in the planes of his face, the line of his cheekbones, was startlingly familiar. We stared at each other for what seemed a long time, and then each of us turned away.

All the way back to the cottage it was his face I saw. Not the sneering menace of the man who'd spoken, but the haunting expression of the man who'd stared so silently.

Fourteen

Danny and I never got to the movies that evening. He called and said a problem had come up at home and he couldn't get away. "I'm sorry, Amy." His voice sounded genuinely regretful, but there was something else in it, too — a hushed, hasty quality, as if he didn't want anyone to hear him talking.

"I'll pick you up tomorrow," he said. "We'll go to the cliff, okay?"

I agreed, trying not to let him hear how disappointed I was at not seeing him that night. I didn't want to be too possessive; I didn't want to *feel* too possessive.

Saturday dawned gray and rainy, with a fine mist blowing in off the ocean. I hoped it would burn off by noon, but when Danny turned into our drive the drizzle had become a downpour, steady and dismal.

"No cliff today," he said ruefully. "What shall we do?"

In the end we just stayed inside, puttering around the cottage and enjoying being together. My father was working in his study, and although he came out to say hello, he wisely left us alone in the living room. Danny built a big fire of apple wood, and I turned the radio on. We sat on the rug in front of the fire and ate the picnic lunch I'd put together the night before.

"This is the life," sighed Danny, stretching out on the hearth, his chin propped in his hands. "I could stay here forever."

"Are you tired?" I searched his face for hints of exhaustion, but there were none. I told myself I was being silly worrying about him. Danny was strong and healthy and young. He could easily handle a full load at North Point and a job.

"No. Just happy." He reached up and caught a long strand of my hair, looping it around his hand and letting it slip through his fingers. "In botany class the other day I kept thinking of you. I had such a clear picture of the way you looked the first time I saw you. You were wearing a yellow tee shirt, and your hair was tied back with a long yellow scarf."

"That's not what I was wearing when I met you," I said indignantly.

"I didn't say when I met you. I said when I first saw you."

I remembered the time I'd felt eyes on me, watching me from the bluffs above the cove. I'd been in the midst of one of my fantasies.

"You *were* watching me," I breathed. "I sensed it, but of course I didn't even know you existed."

"It took me a while to work up my courage and introduce myself."

"Oh, Danny — " I felt almost choked with emotion. The thought that this boy would need courage to meet me was overwhelming. Something was pricking at the back of my mind, insisting on my attention, but then Danny pulled my hair gently and my face came down to his and we kissed. It was a soft kiss, and loving. I knew that with my father in the house there'd be none of the passionate, long kisses that left me weak and trembling, and I was both sorry and relieved.

I cupped my hand around Danny's cheek and looked down at him, and that's when it hit me. The line of the stranger's cheekbones, the set of his eyes — the whole look of him — had been familiar because he looked like Danny! In that moment I felt convinced that the man was Danny's father. He could be no one else. Why Mr. Morgan had come back after so many years I couldn't imagine, but I was as sure I'd seen him on the rocks yesterday as I was sure of anything in my life.

I mumbled something about getting some grapes from the fridge and went to the kitchen. I leaned my head against the door frame and thought. It was clear to me I couldn't just announce it to Danny. He was disturbed enough whenever I so much as *mentioned* his father. On the subject of his family he was like an unbroken horse — if you went too close he reared and ran off, but if you questioned him very gently he would give short, guarded answers.

When I came back, a plate of purple grapes and

some cheese and crackers balanced in my arms, I asked, very casually: "That problem at home? Is everything all right now?"

"Yeah," said Danny, looking into the fire. "No big deal."

"You never told me about your other brothers and sisters," I said, selecting a grape and popping it into my mouth. "Except for Maggie, are they all older?"

"Two are. I have a married sister in Sacramento, and a brother in the merchant marine."

"Is he much older than you? Does he look like you?" I was grasping at straws. I wanted the man I had seen to be anyone but Danny's father, because there was no logical explanation for Mr. Morgan to come back, after all these years.

"He's twenty-one. He looks like my mother — not at all like me." He turned over on his back and looked up at me, his brows knit. "Why so many questions?"

"Just curious. When you care about someone, it's nice to know about them." I rushed on, before I lost my nerve. "And the other one? Is it a brother or a sister?"

Danny stirred uneasily. "Neal. He's seventeen, right between Maggie and me. And don't ask why you haven't seen him at school. Neal lives with an aunt, over near Grosvenor."

His tone had become low and sulky, and I realized he wanted to close the subject.

"Neal was in reform school when he was fourteen. They called him an incorrigible youth." Danny laughed bitterly. "My mother visits him once a week and sends money for his upkeep. He was more than she could handle. I stopped visiting him a year ago."

"I'm sorry," I said softly.

"Me, too. Let's talk about something else."

For the rest of the afternoon we played Scrabble and lazed around. Once my father popped out of his study and asked Daniel if he'd care to see an interesting slide and Danny, the would-be marine biologist, followed him enthusiastically, leaving me alone to think. The foghorn had started up, and it was a perfect backdrop for my gloomy thoughts.

It seemed to me that Danny's father, by deserting his family, had ruined two lives and scarred two others. I remembered the face I had studied yesterday and tried to read into it the cruelty and indifference I attributed to Danny's father, but all I remembered was the sadness.

Danny stayed to have supper with us that night, and then he had to leave to work the late shift at the lumber mill. I walked him out to the truck to say good-bye. The rain had stopped, but fog lay thick and stifling everywhere. The foghorn was moaning ceaselessly, and high seas boomed into the cove like a giant battering ram.

"Drive carefully," I said, slipping into his arms and kissing him lightly. "Please be careful, Danny. You can't see two feet in front of you."

"Always worrying," he said teasingly. "Nag, nag, nag." He kissed the tip of my nose. "I know every inch of these roads, remember?" And then he jumped into the pickup, turned around in the drive, and drove off. The fog swallowed the taillights up before he had reached the end of the drive, and I turned back, feeling lonely and yet reassured. Whatever was happening, Danny loved me and I loved him. Together, we'd be able to triumph over any stumbling blocks the outside world set up for us.

That's what I thought, and I continued to think it until the middle of the next week, when my world fell apart. Danny called to say he wouldn't be able to see me that weekend. He didn't give any explanation or even say he was sorry, and when I asked what had happened he simply said he couldn't talk and would explain later. By Thursday, when I'd heard nothing, I called the Morgan number. Maggie answered.

"He's not at home," she said. "Sorry." For a moment I thought she really did feel sorry, and then the phone was replaced and the line went dead.

He was waiting for me Friday, after school. It was so unusual to see him outside the school I had to look twice to make sure it was Danny. He was wearing old jeans and a flannel shirt. I ran up to him, trying not to show how relieved and happy I was, but something in his expression stopped me. "I had to talk to you," he said. "Let me drive you home."

"You're supposed to be at the lumber mill," I said stupidly.

He shrugged. "I'll have to be late this once."

We drove in silence nearly all the way, and when he pulled off the road a mile above Crozier's Cottage I felt my mouth go dry with fear. Whatever he had to tell me couldn't be good.

"I've been thinking a lot about us," he said. He stared straight ahead, over the steering wheel.

"We're getting in too deep, Amy. You're too young to know your own mind. You ought to be dating lots of guys, enjoying your senior year. I've enjoyed knowing you, but I think we should cool it for a while. You're a sensible girl. I'm sure you understand."

I stared at his profile, at the black lashes concealing his eyes from me, at the sensitive mouth, capable of such tender kisses, now set firmly against me. I couldn't believe what I was hearing.

"I don't understand," I said, trying to keep my voice level. "You know I don't want to go out with anyone else. I know my mind as well as you do."

"Don't make it any harder for me, Amy. Please."

"I love you," I said desperately. "If you've met someone else at North Point, just tell me! I deserve honesty from you, Danny! Don't give me a song and dance about being too young. Tell me the truth."

"Okay," said Danny. "Here's the truth. There's no one else, but I want out. I just want out. Is that clear enough for you, Amy?"

"Clear as crystal," I said bitingly. "I misjudged you, Daniel Morgan. I'm glad I found out what you are really like before it was too late." I got out of the truck then and walked off toward Crozier's Cottage. I kept my head very high and my back straight. Right up until the last moment I hoped he'd run after me, tell me it wasn't true, but I heard the sound of the truck reversing and knew he was driving off. When I couldn't hear the sound of the motor any longer I let the tears come. I just put one foot in front of the other, walking blindly, tears streaming down my face. There was a terrible pain in my chest, and I understood what people meant when they said "a broken heart." I could actually feel the pain, and I imagined it would never go away. Later, wave after wave of humiliation and anger washed over me. Danny had duped me, amused himself with me for the summer just the way Miranda had implied he would. Now he had a whole world of college girls to choose from, and I was cast aside as casually as if I were a disposable towel.

I have a theory about having your heart broken. I think the anger comes just so you can deal with the pain. It's easier to be angry than to feel empty and lost — at least you can focus on something other than your own misery! Unfortunately, the anger fades, too, and you're left with the ache of missing the very person who's been rotten to you.

At my lowest point I thought about how I'd see him when he came to collect his mother. At least I'd be able to lay eyes on him, even if I hid behind a curtain to do it. On Sunday night, even this humble glimmer of hope was taken from me.

"I'll have to look for another housekeeper, squirrel," my father said absently. He looked up. "Aren't you well, Amy? You've looked so pale all weekend."

"I'm fine, Daddy. Why can't we continue with Mrs. Morgan?"

"She called earlier. It seems her arthritis is acting up badly. She won't be able to come here anymore."

"I didn't know she had arthritis," I said.

"Neither did I. It's a shame."

And so, all in one dismal weekend, my father lost his housekeeper and I lost the only boy I'd ever loved.

Fifteen

I knew that by the weekend everybody in school would be aware that Danny and I had broken up, because that's when we would have been going to Jerry Bell's party after the first football game of the season. I planned to stay home all weekend, gathering strength for the pitying glances that would come my way the following Monday. I'd need special strength to tolerate the look of triumph I imagined gleaming in Miranda's eyes.

When I got home that day, Mrs. Pearson, the new housekeeper, was there. She was an elderly woman, tiny and efficient, who darted about with the quick pecking movements of a bird. Although she was at least sixty, she seemed more carefree than Mrs. Morgan ever had. She drove a snappy little red Toyota and whistled when she rolled out pastry dough.

"Hi there, dearie!" she called when she heard me shut the front door. "There's a storm brewing, did you know? It's heading down the coast from Oregon."

By the time she left, at five, the air was unnaturally thick and heavy. The water in the cove was smooth and unruffled, but the ocean looked somehow oily and dark and threatening. Gulls were wheeling over the cottage, screeching and settling nervously, only to flap off again.

For the first time in weeks, I felt uneasy in Crozier's Cottage. I didn't like being alone with a storm coming on; logic told me there was nothing to fear, but logic had nothing to do with it. Ever since I'd met Danny, I'd come to love it here. All the things I'd found menacing and alien had become beautiful when I explored them with him. Now that he was gone I felt much as I had in that first week. The Cottage, with all its dim recesses and bleak views of the ocean, was a gloomy, sad place. I remembered the unlucky fortunes of those who had lived here, and repressed a shiver. If I listened carefully, the wind now whistling down the chimney, the sea stirring against the shore, sounded like one long sigh of misery.

It was growing dark, and I hadn't turned on any of the lamps. The first drops of rain were pattering down on the slate roof, and it was only a matter of minutes before the foghorn would groan into action. I moved toward the living room to switch on the lights and build a fire to welcome my father home, but as I stood in the doorway a cold wave of fear washed over me. I felt it as you'd feel an actual wave wash over your toes in a wintry sea. The room was in almost total darkness, and I forced myself to move toward the light switch. My hands scraped over the wall, searching for the switch, and found nothing. My throat was thick with a nameless fear, the kind I could remember from childhood when I'd awakened from a nightmare I couldn't quite remember. Just as my fingers made contact with the switch, I knew what it was. I was afraid I wasn't alone in Crozier's Cottage. I was afraid my questing fingers would touch a sleeve, a hand, in the darkness.

Light flooded the room then, and I could see I was quite alone. I knelt down at the hearth and got kindling together for a fire, and when I'd finished that task I drew the curtains across all the windows. I wanted to go from room to room, turning on the lights, but I knew, without wanting to admit it, that I was afraid to leave the safety of the living room. I sat for nearly two hours in that room, waiting to hear the sound of my father's car in front, and when at last it came I wanted to cry with relief.

At dinner, I decided to tell my father about Danny and me. I was afraid to postpone it much longer, because the longer I waited the more painful it would be.

"I'm sorry, Amy," he said. "I know how hurt you must feel, but try to see it his way. It's hard for a young man to hold down a job and take a full load of credits. So much is expected of Danny on a full scholarship. He doesn't dare ease up or take a break, the way some of them do. I admire him."

I started to protest, to tell my father that Danny's studies had nothing to do with our splitting. I had understood his obligations better than anyone. I had encouraged him right down the line! I opened my mouth to say all this and then shut it again. What did it matter? The important thing was that Danny was gone from my life. If he'd met another girl at North Point, my father was bound to notice. I preferred not to know.

All that evening the storm grew wilder, raging down the coast and howling over Klamath Heights until the noise was almost deafening. My father, who loved a good storm, insisted we put on our raincoats and watch the waves in the cove from the bluff. The wind was so fierce I clung to his arm for fear I'd be blown over the side.

"Look!" he shouted gleefully. "Isn't it magnificent, Amy?"

The waves must have been ten feet high, and they hurled themselves into my gentle little cove as if trying to destroy it forever. The white of the bursting foam seemed to glow in the darkness, and several times the spray flew high enough to hit our faces. What my father found magnificent I thought violent and frightening. It was too dark to see up the coast, and I was grateful. If the cove had been transformed to this raging cauldron, I hated to imagine what it was like at the foot of the cliff.

The spot where I had encountered the three men would be totally under water now. *It's dangerous to walk here. Don't you know that?* "Let's go inside," I shouted, my voice swallowed up by the wind.

"Daddy," I said, when we were safely indoors, "have you ever seen anyone on the beach here?"

"No. Aside from you and the gulls, it seems to be empty."

"I saw three men the other day. It wasn't the first time I'd seen them, either." And then, omitting only the man's warning to me and my suspicions about one of them being Danny's father, I told my father about my peculiar meeting. His brow furrowed in thought, and he nodded.

"Odd," he said. "I wouldn't have thought of it, but once when I was on a field trip — " He laughed. "Actually, there's nothing odd about it. I saw them through the binoculars, three of them. They were in a dinghy. Amateur divers, probably, because they seemed to be wearing wetsuits. I couldn't really see at that distance."

"Divers? At this time of year? What would they be looking for?"

"Almost anything. Old salvage, wrecks of ships. Maybe they were looking for treasure. Amateur divers will spend days in a rich location, just on the off-chance of finding something. They're probably long gone by now, squirrel."

"Where did you see them?"

"They appeared to be just beneath the bird cliff at the point. The way the coast doubles back on itself, they wouldn't be visible from any place except directly above."

So my father had discovered Danny's special place. I should have known — it was a naturalist's paradise. "Those cliffs are dangerous, Daddy," I said. "You mustn't walk alone there, you know. Especially not if there's mist or fog."

"Now who's acting like a parent?" My father kissed my cheek and went off to his study to grade papers. Next semester, Danny would be in one of his classes, but for now I didn't have to worry. My father might be absentminded, but he was very sensitive about my feelings. He would never mention Danny to me again, not unless I brought him up first, and that was just how I wanted it. I went to bed determined to erase all thoughts of Daniel Morgan from my mind.

Just before I dropped off to sleep, a procession of ghosts seemed to pass through my consciousness. They trooped along in a line, and although I couldn't see any of their faces I knew who they were. The tallest was Jacob Crozier, who had built the cottage for his bride and then died in the war in France. Behind him were his son, who had drowned, and the son's first wife, who had wandered too close to the edge of the cliff. I thought Daniel's great-great-grandfather was among them, too, and the crew of that ill-fated ship. I heard Mrs. Morgan's voice saying: *I do believe there are places that are unlucky, though. They don't start out that way, but if too many tragedies occur . . .*

Amazingly, I had no nightmares that night. I slept through the rest of the storm as deeply as if I'd been drugged. When I woke up the sky was gray and clear, as if the howling winds had washed all color from it forever.

Sixteen

Miranda was elected Harvest Queen, surprising no one. I had cast my vote for Joanne, and my only wish was not to be involved in any of the festivities. When Lisa told me the runners-up would act as Miranda's court I kind of blew my top.

"I'm not going to be in Miranda's court," I said acidly. "I'm just not interested in any of it."

Lisa and Joanne exchanged significant glances.

On Monday Miranda stopped me in school and said, "Is it true you dumped Danny?" Her eyes were shining with an emotion I couldn't quite figure. Certainly it was triumphant, as I'd imagined it would be, but I soon realized she thought she'd triumphed over Danny, not me.

"It was mutual," I said. "Nobody *dumped* anybody, Miranda. We just made a decision not to see each other anymore."

She caught her full lower lip between her teeth and then grinned wickedly. "You can't fool me," she said in a low voice. "Danny was crazy about you!" She practically hugged herself with glee. "I'm so glad, Amy! He had it coming. It serves him right."

I stared at her, astonished. I had never seen Miranda look so happy, or so girlish. She imagined I'd made Danny suffer, and she was in absolute ecstasy. I was just thinking what a monster she was when she asked me if I'd like to go to the Timber after school. It was the first time she'd ever been remotely friendly to me, and all because I'd helped her get revenge on Danny. Or so she thought.

"No thanks, Miranda," I said coolly. I walked off, leaving her puzzled for a change. Our positions were reversed.

It wasn't much of a triumph, though. I would have given anything to ask how she knew that Danny had been crazy about me. Had he told her? Had they spent time together I didn't know about? Now I'd be tormented by jealousy, too, and I hardly needed that.

Two things happened — not very important by themselves — that made me begin to wonder about Danny's reasons for breaking up. I'd gone along assuming the worst, thinking I wasn't really interesting enough for him, wondering if I'd done something wrong, believing I'd misjudged him and accusing him of being shallow, fickle, heartless.

The first thing that made me wonder was Maggie Morgan's strange appearance. Her vivid face was pale and colorless, and there were dark circles under her eyes. She didn't laugh with her friends anymore, but sat sullen and withdrawn, not speaking to anybody. Even though I knew I'd be snubbed, I risked talking to her at lunch one day.

"How's your mother, Maggie?"

She looked up from her paper container of orange juice, her blue eyes tired and expressionless. "Okay," she said.

"Her arthritis?" I prompted. "Is it better?"

"My mother doesn't have arthritis," said Maggie. "You must be thinking of someone else."

And that was the second. Somehow it was all tied together — Danny's leaving me, Mrs. Morgan's quitting, Maggie's listless behavior. Something was very wrong at the Morgan house. I saw the face of the stranger on the beach and knew, without any doubt at all, that my original hunch had been right. Danny's father had returned to Klamath after ten years, and he was at the root of all our troubles. Danny himself hadn't known it the afternoon I'd questioned him about his family, but he'd certainly known it the day he said we had to stop seeing each other.

I waited two days to act, partly because I didn't know what to do, and partly because I needed my father's car. On his day off, I asked if I could borrow it and drive into Klamath to visit Joanne. I set off, my hands clutching the steering wheel until the knuckles were white. I didn't approve of prying into other people's business, but I had to do something. I had never seen Danny's house, but I knew where it was. I made a semicircle around the lake and turned off at a long lane that branched up into the hills. The houses here weren't like Miranda's pretty, white Colonial, or even Joanne's and Lisa's neat little frame houses. They were rundown and shabby, and some of them were little more than cabins. An old yellow dog ran yelping out from a weedy garden and followed along behind the car, darting almost under the wheels.

At last the houses thinned out and there were only woods, birch and pine and poplar, stretching away from the road. It had narrowed until it was little more than a dirt track, and I was beginning to think I'd overlooked the house when I saw the mailbox to my right. It was painted green and nearly hidden by an overgrown hedge, but it said MORGAN. I left the car there, in the lane, and walked up the path toward the house.

It was a fairly large frame house, not as neglected as some of the others I'd seen, but shabby. You could tell that whoever lived there tried to keep it nice, but lost a running battle. Storms had weathered the wood and peeled the paint, and the roof had been repaired with shingles that didn't match the rest. No dogs ran out to greet me. It was very silent. Only the wind moving in the branches of a large pine disturbed the utter quiet. I could see the ruts of the pickup's tires in the drive, but of course Daniel would never be here at this hour. I couldn't have come if there was any chance of seeing him.

I walked up on the wooden porch and searched for the bell, but there was none, so I tapped on the door. No answer. I stood for a while, idly noting that the poplars were turning golden and red in the October sun, and then I knocked again, harder. Some tiny noise inside alerted me, and then I heard the sound of scuffing footsteps, and Mrs. Morgan was peering out at me. At first I barely recognized her. She seemed to have aged ten years, and there was something of the sullen, frightened look about her I'd noticed in her daughter.

"Hello, Mrs. Morgan," I said, trying to sound bright and casual. "I was running some errands for my father and I thought I'd stop by and see how you were."

"That was nice of you, Amy," she said in a low voice that was almost a whisper. "As you can see, I'm not too well."

"Your arthritis?"

"Yes, it's terrible this fall. They say it comes with the changing of the seasons." She continued to stare at me, as if I frightened her. Clearly, she wasn't going to invite me in.

"I only thought . . . I wondered if anything was wrong? I hoped I could help — "

"What could be wrong?" Mrs. Morgan now looked terrified. "What could be wrong, Amy? No, no — everything's fine, except for this stupid arthritis." She made a move as if to close the door. "Thank you for stopping by, Amy. It was kind of you."

One minute more and I'd lose her. "May I have a glass of water?" I asked desperately. "I hate to trouble you, but I'm so thirsty."

Mrs. Morgan opened the door a crack and allowed me in. We were standing in her kitchen, and to my amazement I saw Maggie sitting at the table, doing her homework. She must have heard everything I said, and except for a quick, scornful look in my direction she behaved as if I weren't there. No doubt she thought I'd come looking for Danny. My cheeks burned at the thought, but I couldn't let my pride interfere with my mission. I thought I'd be able to tell, just by setting foot in the Morgan house, if I'd been right. I can't imagine what I expected to find. Certainly not a man's woolen cap, or anything that obvious. I was looking only for some confirmation of my theory, no matter how slender it was. Mrs. Morgan took a glass from the cupboard and filled it with tap water. Then she brought it to me and watched while I drank. There was no invitation to sit down at the kitchen table. In fact, she seemed desperately anxious for me to go.

"Thank you," I said, handing the glass back to her. The whole scene was unreal. Here I was, standing in a kitchen with worn green linoleum on the floor and an oilcloth-covered table. A pot of something simmered on the stove, and an old school clock ticked the time away. It was shabby, but comfortable enough. Why, then, did it seem to me that Maggie and her mother were prisoners here? Why did I sense that what Mrs. Morgan felt was terror?

"You must go now," she said suddenly. "Thank you for coming, Amy, but *you must go.*"

Her tone was so intense I could only obey. I started to tell her that I'd like to visit again sometime to chat with her, but she practically shoved me out the door. Behind her shoulder I saw Maggie, silent as a statue at the table, her head raised as if she heard a sound.

I was just getting into the car when I heard it, too. A car was coming up the lane, and the Morgan women had heard it from a long way off. I sat behind the wheel waiting. I was so sure that I would see the man I'd met on the beach that it was doubly shocking when the old pickup rattled around the bend with Danny at the wheel. I only saw his face for a second before he turned in the drive. His eyes went wide with shock when he recognized me, and his face, beneath the summer tan, became ashen.

I backed halfway down the long lane at breakneck speed, then turned in someone's driveway and drove shakily down to the main road. I had wanted proof that something was wrong at the Morgans', and I'd come away without it, but there are times when you don't need solid proof to know you're right. The atmosphere had been thick with fear and anxiety. I hadn't imagined it.

Near the turnoff for the cliff, I stopped the car and rested my head on the wheel. My father had said he'd seen three men in his binoculars. It was up to me to discover what they were up to. I would come here, alone, in midafternoon, with the binoculars, and do some spying on my own. I had it all planned. I'd tell my father I had a touch of the flu tomorrow and wouldn't be going to school. Then I'd walk up to the point and carefully retrace every step I'd taken with Danny. There would be no danger, so long as I remembered the exact route we'd taken together on those golden afternoons last summer.

I told myself my heart was pounding so hard because of my plans, but I knew it was because of the unexpected glimpse of Danny. The look on his face was one I couldn't forget, no matter how hard I tried.

Seventeen

It rained the next day, and the day after that, so I didn't have to invent a case of flu. I was relieved, because now I wouldn't have to lie to my father. I'd simply go on Saturday, when it would seem perfectly natural. By a really quirky coincidence, though, he managed to make me feel guilty. He came home with a ten-speed bicycle he'd bought for me up at North Point.

"It's nearly new, squirrel," he said. "A student was selling it, and I took one look and thought it would be perfect for you. Now you can get around better when I have the car. You can take it and ride around looking for sketch sites." He looked somehow shy, and quite proud of himself.

"It's beautiful," I said, admiring the cobalt-blue paint job and the sleek gears. "Thank you." I hugged him, feeling ashamed. If the weather cleared by Saturday, I'd be taking the bike on a trip he would never allow, if he knew.

Saturday was one of those perfect Indian summer days when you can almost forget that winter is just around the corner. The sea and sky were as deep a blue as the paint on my new bike, and the sun was blasting away over the coastline as if it thought we were in mid-August. Just beneath the warmth was a tart chill, though, and I dressed warmly, pulling on long knee socks and layering two sweaters over my old flannel shirt. I could always peel away the layers if it got too hot. I made myself two sandwiches, grabbed a pear and some grapes, and stuffed my lunch into a big canvas rucksack, along with a book, *Tess of the D'Urbervilles,* we were reading for English. I draped my father's binoculars over my shoulder, grabbed my sketchbook, and went outside.

My father was in front, examining a small cypress tree that had been uprooted during the storm last week. "Poor *cupressus,*" he said, indicating the ravaged tree. "He's had it, I'm afraid."

"I'm going out sketching," I said airily. "I've got my lunch, and I've borrowed your binoculars. I'll be back by late afternoon." Then I pedaled casually up the drive, hoping he wouldn't find any objection. He waved good-bye, smiling. It was exactly noon.

The bike rode like a dream — even the uphill stretches weren't too bad — and I made excellent time. Inside twenty minutes I'd passed the strange, twisted trees guarding the approach to the upper coast road, and soon I was gliding through that odd, featureless terrain that reminded me of a moonscape. The sun was hot on my shoulders, and I could smell the sea air, even though I couldn't see the water yet. The coast twisted sharply and it was only because the point stuck out farther into the ocean that we were able to see it from Crozier's Cove. The men probably thought they were perfectly safe from prying eyes. I was sure they believed they'd scared me off, and anyway, it would never occur to them I'd go farther than the beach leading from our cottage.

When I rounded the final curve and saw the Pacific spread out before me it was like returning to the scene of a dream. There was one moment of blinding nostalgia when I remembered the first time Danny had brought me here, and then I commanded myself to banish any romantic thoughts and get down to business. I wheeled the bike a little way into the gorse and pushed it down behind some springy bushes where it would be safe, and then I set out across that endless gray-green shoulder of land, taking the path Danny had shown me.

Even now, I didn't look forward to the part that had always frightened me. With Daniel to guide me I'd grown used to it, but alone I knew I'd have to call up all my courage to walk that tightrope trail over the drop. When I could see it, just below, my breathing came faster and I felt my palms sweating slightly. Viewed from above, it looked like a thread stretched over the chasm, but just beyond lay the safety of the rock ledge. I could hear the birds very faintly, and as the path wound down toward the perilous thread the sound of their myriad voices grew more distinct.

I thought of resting before inching along the hated stretch, but I knew the longer I waited the more frightened I would become. I adjusted my rucksack for perfect balance and started out. The gorse was a little slippery from the rain, and I could feel the soles of my sneakers sliding dangerously. I wished I had taken my shoes off, but I couldn't stop now. I kept my eyes dead ahead, on the ledge, and tried to ignore the yawning emptiness to my left. I knew it was there, could sense the dizzying blue nothingness of pure air, could hear the sea pounding far below. When my feet touched the rock of the ledge I gave a huge sigh of relief that was almost a sob. I sank down to rest for a moment, and then I gathered my things and went out to the edge, to the comfortable hollow where Danny had first kissed me.

I spread one of my sweaters on the rock and lay on my stomach, propping my chin in my hands. The birds were screeching all around me in their penthouse, and the sea boiled over the jagged rocks hundreds of feet below me, but here I felt safe. There was no movement on the rocks or in the water beyond, and when I scanned the area with my binoculars I saw nothing. Never mind — I planned to stay all afternoon, and I felt sure my patience would be rewarded. I ate some grapes and flipped through my sketchbook, sticking my tongue out at the terrible self-portrait I had done so long ago. Further along I came to a sketch of Mrs. Morgan, and a funny one of Joanne on the parallel bars in gym. I had ripped all the sketches of Danny from the book soon after our break-up, but they were in my bureau drawer at home, shoved under a pile of pajamas. I couldn't bear to throw them away.

I managed to use up some time drawing a fat-breasted bird who perched inquisitively near me for some time, and then I ate one of my sandwiches. Every few minutes I would look through the binoculars, but all I saw was seabirds. At last I took my copy of *Tess of the D'Urbervilles* out and settled down to read a chapter or two.

I liked Tess and felt sorry for her, detesting the man she loved for spurning her so cruelly. Her fierceness and pride reminded me of myself, somehow, and that made it all the sadder to read of her suffering. I tried to read Danny into the part of Angel Clare, or Alec, but Angel was too holier-than-thou and Alec too wicked to remind me of him.

The sun was so warm on my shoulders it was making me sleepy, so I ate my pear and tried to imagine what Miranda would think of Tess. Miranda wouldn't understand Hardy's heroine at all. She'd think Tess was a fool and despise her for loving a man who had turned his back on her. I remembered the look of triumph in Miranda's eyes when she'd thought I'd ditched Danny. *Good for you. He deserves it. He had it coming.* Miranda would never suffer, because she was heartless and selfish and cared only for herself. In a way I envied her.

My thoughts turned around lazily, mixing with the cries of the birds and the hissing and pounding of the sea, and before I knew it I had dropped off to sleep. I dreamed I was Tess, but then suddenly Miss Oates, the art teacher, was saying: *You mustn't walk alone, Amy. Don't walk alone.*

When I woke up the sun was much lower, and my shoulders were no longer warm. I had a cramp in my arm and for a moment I didn't know where I was. There was an instant of horror when I looked down and saw the foam breaking on the rocks, but then I knew, and I was instantly alert. It was four o'clock, and I had slept for almost two hours! I stretched my cramped legs out and started to gather my things together. I was putting *Tess* back into my rucksack when some very tiny movement at the very edge of my vision caught my attention. Something, or somebody, was moving about on the rocks below. I fumbled for the binoculars and brought them into focus. At first I could see nothing, and then I realized they weren't on the rocks, but in the water. I was staring directly down at them. They were in a dinghy, in the open water beyond the jagged teeth of the rocks. One sat in the stern and as I watched, the other two clambered up over the bow. They were wearing rubber wetsuits. Even with the binoculars, I couldn't see them too clearly, but the man in the dinghy was staring out across the water so that I had a perfect view of his face.

Even the line of his chin was Daniel's, and the dark, level eyebrows. I couldn't stop watching him, marveling at the resemblance, but where Danny's face was fresh and unlined, this man's was marked by signs of bitterness and suffering.

As soon as the other two had flung themselves on board, the man rowed back toward the rocks. I held my breath, sure they would be dashed to splinters as each heaving swell brought them closer, and then they just vanished. There was no other word for it. One moment they were there, and the next they were gone.

I kept the binoculars pressed to my eyes, watching the spot where they had disappeared, and in five minutes I picked them up again. The two in wetsuits were now dressed in the same dark clothes they'd worn the day I met them, and all three of them were talking rapidly. It looked as if they were having an argument.

Common sense told me they'd tied the dinghy up in a tiny inlet or water cave. Mrs. Morgan had said the coast was honeycombed with them. But I couldn't imagine where they were going now! I had lost all sense of danger, because I was too absorbed in studying the face I felt sure belonged to Danny's father. I couldn't keep my eyes from him, and that's how I made my first big mistake. I saw him give a start and look up angrily, and it seemed he was staring directly at me. It was so eerie, I swung the binoculars to the other men, and that's when my heart nearly stopped.

The others were looking up, too, but what made me go cold with terror was the flash from the late afternoon sun as it reflected from another pair of binoculars. One of the men was staring at me, just as I had been staring at Danny's father, in close-up. My fingers felt glued to the binoculars, and before I could drop them and roll away out of sight, the man dropped his glass and smiled into my eyes. It was the same smile I had seen on the beach, and it held a dreadful promise. *Don't you know it's dangerous to walk here?*

Gasping, I wriggled into my rucksack and ran, crouching low, over the ledge. There was no time to gather courage for the walk along the narrow trail. I went lurching and slipping along, sure at any moment I would lose my footing and pitch over the side. I ran back all the way to my bicycle, panting and slipping in the gorse, and just as I was about to pull it up from its hiding place I realized there was no rush. There was no way the men could get to me from where they were, not unless they were mountain goats. I stared back at where I had been, and felt the familiar chill as I noticed the sea mist beginning to drift in. It was late October now, and the sun would set soon and quickly. The mist would cover everything.

I pedaled back as fast as I could, the memory of that threatening smile filling my thoughts. At least my face had been covered, mostly, by the binoculars. They couldn't have got a good look at me, really. I might have been anyone at all.

I was so glad to see the lights in Crozier's Cottage, and my father's slightly worried face, that I nearly broke down and told him everything. It wasn't until we were having dinner together that the real horror struck me.

"Get any good sketches, *sciurus*? It was a beautiful day. Amy? Is anything wrong? Aren't you feeling well?"

I mumbled something about how the flu was going around and pushed my plate away. In my haste to leave the ledge, I'd left my sketchbook behind. I could see it, lying open at the edge of the cliff, its pages blowing in the night wind. Even more important, I could see the cover, with my name and address firmly inked in, so that if I ever lost it a stranger could return it to me. If the night was calm, I might still be safe, but if the winds that whipped around the point had started soon after I left . . . if they were blowing out to sea . . .

That was the worst vision of all — my book, with my name and address, blowing down to the men below as neatly as a calling card.

Eighteen

"The library?" Lisa looked puzzled. "What's there?"

"Books," I said smartly. "I have to pick up some books for my father." This seemed to satisfy her, and she and Rick left me in peace. I didn't mean to turn them off, but the kids who'd been my friends, with their casual fun and devil-may-care attitude, seemed as irrelevant to me now as the library did to Lisa. I was caught up in something far more serious, and I had no time for Cokes at the Timber.

Two days had passed since my disastrous watch on the cliffs, and I'd been stretched tight as a drum, my nerves on edge, ever since. Sunday had been rainy and misty, and even if I could have safely gone to the rock ledge it would have been impossible. My father had come down with the flu, for real, and I had spent all day taking him soup and tea and bringing him papers to grade from his study. He was still at home today, and I had been allowed to take the car to school.

Parking in back of the library, I tried to imagine the fate of my sketchbook. The wind had risen, certainly, and I thought it had been blown safely out to sea, where it could do me no harm. My nervousness now was for a different reason. I'd begun to think that maybe the whole business was something I'd cooked up in my overheated brain. Klamath and Klamath Heights were full of Morgans — even the librarian was related to Mrs. Morgan — and the man I'd seen could have been a harmless fisherman or salvage diver distantly related. I burned with humiliation when I recalled my impetuous raid on the Morgan house. Probably what I'd read as fear on Danny's mother's face was sheer embarrassment for me. I shuddered most of all when I recalled the look on Danny's face. He thought I was chasing him.

"What can I do for you today?" The friendly librarian was smiling eagerly. There were only four people in the place, and I guess she was glad to be of help to someone.

"I wondered if there were any old books about the area," I said. "I'm doing a report in school, and I thought I'd check it out."

"I'm afraid you'll have to be more specific," the librarian said kindly. "Were you interested in books on early settlers? The lumbering industry? Spanish land grants?"

"Shipping, maybe. I mean old wrecks along the coast."

She brightened immediately and showed me three books she thought would interest me. One was a standard history of shipwrecks along the northern Pacific coast, and one was a specific account of a wreck some fifty miles north of us. The third one, though, was a gold mine. It was called *Full Fathom Five — Klamath Point,* and promised to be every bit as spooky as anything Mrs. Morgan had ever told me. The librarian told me it was written by a Klamath resident in the nineteenth century and was very valuable. It was practically falling apart, and I promised to treat it gently.

"That book is for reference only, dear. I'm afraid you won't be able to take it with you."

That's how I happened to sit in the library until closing when, with a start, I realized it was six o'clock and my father would be having a fit. I hadn't even been aware of the time passing because the book was so fascinating.

Mrs. Morgan had been right. For centuries the waters beneath the point had been a ships' graveyard. In the fifteenth century a Russian ship, sailing from Sitka to San Francisco, had run aground and sunk with a cargo full of precious furs. Spanish galleons had smashed to bits on those rocks from the sixteenth to eighteenth centuries, and one of them, the *Santa Rosario,* had gone down with a fortune in pieces of eight which had never been recovered. From sailing ships to steamers to coast guard cutters, the sea showed no mercy. Even in the author's own time a tragedy had occurred, and reading on I found it was the wreck Mrs. Morgan had told me about. Augustus Riley was the name of the man who had survived.

Down through the years, professional and amateur divers had tried to pry that treasure in gold from the ocean's bed, but no one had ever found anything but the skeletons of the ships. "Even in these modern times," wrote the author in 1878, "ships would do well to give the murderous rocks at Klamath Point a wide berth. Why tempt fate?"

Why, indeed? I thought as I returned the book and apologized to the librarian for keeping her. "You said you were Maudie Morgan's cousin," I said. "How is she feeling?"

"I didn't know she was sick," said the librarian. "Maudie's moody, you know. I've known her since we were girls. My sister, Clare, and her ex-husband, David, were brother and sister."

David Morgan. I had never heard his name before. The librarian was the first person I had ever heard refer to him without sounding angry or self-conscious. "Well," she said, dismissing me and glancing at the clock, "that was all a long time ago."

I drove home, thinking about Spanish galleons and pieces of eight, and a man named David who had once loved a girl named Maud. It seemed improbable that my weird scenario had any truth to it. Grown men didn't fool around with little dinghies, trying to recover treasure lost three hundred years ago. It was preposterous.

Mrs. Pearson was waiting for me when I returned, coat and hat on and foot tapping with impatience.

"I'm sorry," I said. "I got held up at the library."

"I didn't want to leave your father alone when he was doing so poorly," she said accusingly. She winked. "I think he'll be better by the day after tomorrow. Men are such children when they're sick."

She darted out to her little Toyota, but just as she was about to climb in she wheeled around. "Someone left a package for you," she called. "I didn't hear a car drive up, but I found it leaning against the door when I shook the rug out." She cocked her head. "It's funny, because generally you can hear a car out here a mile away. It's on the dining room table."

It was wrapped in brown paper and taped closed, but it could only be my sketchbook. I picked it up gingerly, as if it might explode. AMY HOLLIS was printed in block capitals on the front of the package. Nothing else. I opened the package and drew my sketchbook out. There was no message or note enclosed. I flipped through it rapidly, watching the familiar images fly past, but no sheet of paper fell out. I was aware of the unnatural coldness of my fingers, and of the words echoing in my head. *Generally you can hear a car out here a mile away.*

Of course, there had been no car, but I couldn't tell Mrs. Pearson that. I couldn't tell anybody. The person who had delivered my sketchbook had walked up the beach, past the rocks and into my own private cove. He had climbed the steps in the bluff and left it, leaning, against my own front door. It was his way of telling me he could find me any time he liked. He was playing with me, trying to warn me off one last time.

All my safe little theories fell apart again, and I was back to square one. The men I had seen may not have been searching for Spanish doubloons, but they were doing something sinister, and I had seen them. Worse, they had seen me. I knew, somehow, that it was the man with the menacing, cruel smile who had brought my book. He looked like the sort of person who might enjoy frightening people.

I heard my father calling to me from his bedroom, and I put the sketchbook down on the dining room table and went up to him. He was sitting up in bed, a glass of ginger ale on the table next to him and a tray containing tiny animal bones on his lap. I was used to such sights. Generally they made me smile, but tonight I was too afraid to think of anything but myself.

"How are you, Daddy? I'm sorry I was late."

"Think nothing of it, Amy. This woodchuck skeleton is quite interesting, don't you think? He appears to have had an abnormally large skull."

"Can I get you anything?"

"No, squirrel. I have a raging headache. I'm going to try to sleep it off so I can get back to work tomorrow. I hope you won't mind making yourself a sandwich for supper."

"Daddy — " I hesitated. It was now or never. I felt I was in too deep, and I needed to tell him about the strange events that so puzzled and frightened me. He looked up, and I could see how flushed and feverish he was. His bright eyes were dulled, and two red spots burned in each of his cheeks. Now was definitely not the time. I would wait until he was better. If I stammered out my bizarre story, it would only sound like something his fever had produced. I removed the tray of bones, plumped up his pillow, and brought him a fresh glass of ginger ale. His temperature was 102°. "Get some sleep, Daddy," I said, and tiptoed out of the room.

Then I went around the house, making sure every door and window was locked firmly. As I was drawing the curtains across the bay window that looked over the cove, I had an unpleasant thought. What if the man was watching me, concealed in the curve of the bluff?

If he had managed to leave my sketchbook at the front door while my father and Mrs. Pearson were inside, there was nothing he couldn't do.

Nineteen

I felt a sharp elbow in my side and I was jolted awake. Confused and embarrassed, I stared stupidly up at Mrs. McAllister, who was regarding me with displeasure.

"English class is not the appropriate place to catch up on your sleep, Amy," she said. "I'm surprised at you."

"I'm sorry," I mumbled, and the class rippled with laughter. Joanne, who had awakened me, shot me a look of sympathy.

"I asked what you thought was Tess's chief character defect," said Mrs. McAllister, "but obviously you didn't hear. Miranda? Would you care to comment?"

"She's really out of it," drawled Miranda, referring to both Tess and me. Miranda went on to explain that Tess was stupid to pine over a dull guy like Angel Clare. "With her looks she should have been able to make something of herself, but she was just too dumb."

"A very interesting assessment," said Mrs. McAllister drily. "I'm sure Thomas Hardy didn't intend his readers to see it in quite that light."

By the end of the period I could feel my head growing heavy again. I'd had almost no sleep the night before, and my eyes felt like hot cinders. Joanne fell into step with me and gave me a worried look.

"You look sick, Amy," she said. "Maybe you caught your Dad's flu."

I shook my head. "I just didn't sleep much last night."

"Thinking about Danny?"

I almost gasped. It was kind of an unspoken rule between us that Danny's name was never mentioned, and I felt betrayed. "No," I said, "not at all. I was finishing *Tess.*" This, of course, was a lie, but I couldn't tell Joanne that I'd sat up in my bedroom listening for sounds of an intruder. Each noise in the nighttime hours at Crozier's Cottage made my heart thud. I imagined that the sighing of the wind, the cries of the gulls, the creaks and groans an old house makes, were warnings. I half expected to hear footsteps ascending the stairs to my room, and finally I'd wedged a straight-back chair beneath my doorknob the way I'd seen it done in movies. Not until the first pale light of dawn had crept in between the curtains did I fall asleep, and then, when the alarm clock shrieked at seven I woke up with a cry. It had not been a restful night.

"I saw him last night," said Joanne. "I thought

you'd want to know." She stared at me. "Are you sure you're okay?"

"Saw who?" My lips felt thick, my tongue dry.

"*Danny*. He came into the hardware store just before it closed. I was buying some epoxy glue for my mother, and Danny came in. He looked kind of strange — not his usual, friendly self. I thought he wasn't going to speak to me, but he was waiting for me outside when I left. He asked me how you were."

"How too, too kind of him," I said sarcastically, hoping Joanne wouldn't notice the flush spreading over my face.

"I said you were fine, but he kept asking questions, you know? It was as if he couldn't hear enough about you. Finally I said, kind of flip, I'd give you his regards." She frowned. "He grabbed my arm and said, 'No — don't do that. Don't mention that you saw me.' He was so *intense*. He almost frightened me. I had to promise I wouldn't say anything, but I knew I'd have to tell you."

"Why?" My heart was beating hard and suddenly I didn't feel sleepy anymore.

"Don't you see? He still cares about you, Amy. It was written all over his face."

The bell rang then and I had to go to French class. For all I heard there I might as well have been asleep again, because all I could think of was Danny. Was it possible he still cared? My mind was whirling with conflicting emotions, and more than anything I felt confused. Everything was confusing me lately, and when that happens you begin to doubt your ability to see things as they are.

I went back over all the reversals I'd been through lately. First, I'd been sure that Danny had dumped me, pure and simple, because he was tired of me and wanted to be free at North Point. Then I'd become convinced that something terrible was happening to the Morgan family, something to do with the man I'd seen on the beach. For a while I'd scoffed at my melodramatic imaginings, and then, last night, I'd had proof that I *wasn't* just imagining things. Now, with Joanne's words ringing in my ears, I was more confused. Maybe Danny was having second thoughts. Maybe he'd wanted to break up with me for the reasons I'd originally thought, and now he was regretting it? Perhaps he was too proud to come back to me after he'd been so cruel. What if Danny's behavior had nothing to do with the men in the cove? Their importance receded. I almost wished Joanne had kept her promise to him, because it was doubly painful to be thinking about him like this.

The school day crawled by so slowly it was like torture. When it was over at last and I was driving home in my father's car, I had another thought and almost drove off the road. What if it had been Danny who'd returned my sketchbook? Just because Mrs. Pearson didn't hear the sounds of his truck didn't mean it hadn't been there. He might have parked it up above, on the road, and walked down, not wanting me to notice him if I was home. It would explain his strange behavior with Joanne later that evening, but what did it really mean?

Danny had told me he went to the bird cliff once a week, but I'd forgotten that in my pain at losing him. I had come to think of it as *our* special place, when it had been Danny's long before he even knew me. If he had gone to the cliff and found my sketchbook, it must have been soon after I'd left. He had kept it for several days before returning it. My brain was buzzing with questions, and I felt as if I hadn't slept for a week.

When I got home my father was in his study, wearing his bathrobe and looking much better. "Mail for you, squirrel," he called. "It's in the hall, next to the telephone."

There were two letters, one from Annie in New Jersey, and one in an unfamiliar handwriting, mailed from just up the coast at Hadley. Fingers trembling, I opened the second envelope and found a single sheet of plain paper. On it was written:

> I'm sorry for everything. I don't want it to be like this, Amy. Please meet me at our place Thursday, when you get out of school. Don't call me or try to get in touch with me before then because I have to talk to you in person.
>
> Love, D.

I read it over and over, and finally the words sank in. Danny did still care, and he wanted to explain everything to me. I imagined how hard it had been for him to write the note, and smiled, thinking of how stubborn he could be.

"Anything interesting?" My father was leaning on the door frame, smiling at me indulgently. "What does Anne have to say?"

I slit open the envelope from my sister and handed the letter to Daddy. "You read it," I said. "Read it out loud. I have something in my eye."

It was only Monday, I thought. How on earth could I wait until Thursday? The hours that stretched ahead until I could see Danny seemed endless! I tried to concentrate on Anne's letter, but it was no use. Thursday, and the promise it held, blotted out everything else.

"If it's a girl," read my father, "we've decided to name her Elizabeth Amy. The Big Event could happen any time now. Maybe by the time you read this you'll be an aunt for the second time! We miss you, and hope you're as happy as your letters sound."

"Are you as happy as your letters sound?" my father asked.

"Yes," I said. "I'm very happy." For the first time in weeks, it was true.

"Good," said my father. "I want both my daughters to be happy." He had a funny little smile on his face, and I guessed it was because he was thinking of Anne and her coming baby. Elizabeth had been my mother's name.

Before I went to bed that night, I took the drawings I'd made of Danny out of their hiding place and studied them. I smoothed my fingers over the paper lovingly, and thought how I'd never been able to show in my sketches how handsome he was. As I looked at his face an odd thought popped into my mind. When I'd flipped through my sketchbook yesterday I'd been too upset to really notice anything. I was busy searching for some menacing note — a filthy scrap of paper, say, with the words *Stay away* scrawled on it, or *Mind your own business!* I smiled at my melodramatic imagination, thinking how foolish I'd been to build three rather unpleasant men into a trio of fiends. Still, something told me one of the sketches in my book was missing. I'd noted it mechanically, subconsciously, and ignored it when the terror came. Curious, I picked up the sketchbook and leafed through it slowly. I didn't have to go far. It was the self-portrait, the pathetic, self-pitying sketch I'd done of myself that was missing. It had been neatly torn out.

I thought it odd, because Danny had always disliked it as much as I did. Certainly he didn't want it for himself, even as a memento. And then I realized why he'd taken it. It was Danny's way of telling me that the cold, shy, negative girl who'd sketched herself so full of despair and loneliness was gone forever. She might have come back for a while, during the time we'd been separated, but after next Thursday she'd never be seen again!

Twenty

Who can tell how much trouble could be avoided if we listened to those little warning bells that go off in our minds every so often? Everybody has them — vague, nagging little doubts that tell you to think out a situation before you act. Usually you're too preoccupied by other, happier thoughts, to pay attention to them. And then, of course, it's too late.

The first little bell went off when I noticed the clouds of mist shrouding the coastline on Thursday morning. If it got really foggy, how could Danny expect me to meet him at our special place? I'd been too happy to even consider unimportant things like weather conditions, but now it worried me. He'd always been so protective, so eager to make sure I never went there alone. Then it came to me. Naturally, if there was fog, I'd wait for him at the turnoff in the road. As the day went on, though, the mist burned off and the sun shone so brightly I forgot to be anxious.

I moved through the school day like a robot, barely hearing what the teachers said, staring at the blue skies beyond the windows, and willing the time to pass. It was a quarter to four when I got back to Crozier's Cottage. I changed into jeans and sneakers in record time. By the time I'd ridden on my bike to the point, it would be nearly quarter past. Danny might already be there!

No pickup truck was parked at the turnoff; it was as deserted and silent as ever. I dropped my bike in the scrub bushes at the side of the road. The sun was lower now, but still bright and warm for late October. There wasn't a cloud in the sky. I set off along the path, half-running in my eagerness. What if he hadn't brought the truck? He could have got a ride up to the Heights and walked the rest of the way. He might be waiting for me now.

Before I had time to be afraid or nervous, I was crossing the narrow part. I felt so strong and confident I didn't even hold my breath or clench my teeth, the way I'd always done before. The rock was empty, and although I was disappointed I sat down in the hollow near the edge and prepared to wait. I'd been waiting since Monday, certainly I could wait a few minutes more.

I kept looking out to sea, hoping at any moment to hear Daniel's voice calling to me as he crossed to the rock. Once I thought I heard his voice in the ceaseless crying of the birds, but when I turned, the gray-green shoulder of land behind me was empty. It wasn't quite as warm now, and I was glad I'd brought my down jacket. I huddled inside its warmth, hugging my knees and watching the shadows striping the sea beneath. Far out, a trawler could just be seen on the horizon. Once I looked at my watch, and was astonished to see it was already five. That was when the second warning bell went off. Danny wouldn't let me wait so long, alone, unless something had happened. In another half hour, at most, I'd have to leave. The sun didn't set until later, and up here, so high, there would be light for a long time, but the sea mist began its curling journey upward long before the setting of the sun.

"Danny," I whispered, "come now. Please." And then, since no one could hear me, I called his name out loud. In the ledges along the top of the cliff, the birds became silent, as if my voice had frightened them. Then, with one loud shriek, they started up again. Underneath their racket I could hear the sea pounding with a new insistence. It had grown rougher — the waves that had boiled around the base of the rocks now slammed up vengefully, as if they wanted to batter the cliff to bits. I had purposely refused to look at my watch for a long time, but when I did I saw with shock that it was a quarter to six. Far below, mist was blanketing the shoreline. I couldn't wait any longer. I thought of how the screaming of the birds would sound in the dark, and knew I didn't want to stay another minute.

My legs were cold and cramped and I rubbed them briskly before attempting the walk back over the ledge. My only hope was that I would run into Danny on the other side. He would catch me in his arms and explain why he hadn't come. We would go where it was warm and safe and everything would still be as I had imagined it.

There was a wind now, not strong enough to be dangerous, but strong enough to make me lean my whole body away from it, away from the long drop, when I started over the unprotected path. A shaft of late sun had turned the sea, just for a moment, into liquid gold, and it seemed to blind me. I was inching along like a crab, trying to ignore the fear that was gaining control of me, when it happened.

The shrieking was all around me, the clapping of wings almost touching my face. Before I could think, or even scream, my body acted for me. I threw myself violently to the left, away from the yawning drop, and lay trembling in the grass. *A bird,* my mind told me. It was only a seabird, startled by my foot along the ledge. I was shaking so hard I didn't dare try to get up until the tremors had passed. I lay on my stomach, fingers clutching the undergrowth, my face turned away from the seaward side. Gradually, I felt calmer. I urged myself to get up before I'd totally lost my nerve, and what I saw, ten feet ahead of me along the path, was something straight from a nightmare.

The little warning bells I'd heard before now turned into a screaming siren of alarm, and I had to bite down hard on my fist to keep from joining it. Ahead of me, at the most dangerous part of the narrow path, I saw a man's shoes in the underbrush. Nothing else, just his shoes, but from the angle I knew the man himself was stretched out waiting for me. I saw myself walking innocently into his trap, felt the hands close around my ankles and force me over the edge. I could imagine the horror of that moment, teetering at the brink of the abyss, and then the greater horror of the long fall. I owed my life to that seabird, whose screaming flight must have been as great a surprise to the man as it was to me. The seabird had saved me, but for how long?

I commanded myself to think clearly because now I was fighting for my life. Time enough later to puzzle it all out. Nothing mattered now but getting away. A small, deadly voice told me it was impossible, but I had to ignore that voice because the alternative was death. It seems amazing to me to remember how calmly I considered my choices. The trembling had gone, but a cold lump of fear spread from my stomach and settled over me like a shroud. There was nothing but the fear, and the need to plan. If I went on over the path my fate was sealed. If I ran back, in the other direction, onto the ledge, he would follow me. There would be no way for me to escape him, except over the edge. My only chance lay in the unknown territory behind me, above the path. I thought of that huge, gray-green no-man's land of gorse and scrub. Danny had warned me that it could be dangerous, too. The cliff was eroded deeply from below, and the seemingly safe green humps could be a slippery springboard to death. Still, it was the only direction that didn't mean *instant* death. I couldn't wait much longer here. He would be suspicious; he would come for me.

My only advantage was that he didn't know I'd seen him. I tried to whistle a little tune, so he'd think I was about to rise up from my bed of safety and come toward him, but my lips were so dry that no sound came. Mist was beginning to rise now. I could see small fingers of it reaching over the cliff edge. I thought the mist I had dreaded could be my ally; if only it would thicken and blanket us in drifting white I would be invisible to him. In the meantime, I had to get out of my red down jacket. It made me a perfect target, and if I was going to run for my life I wanted every advantage. Silently, I peeled it off, shivering in the sudden cold, and regarded the shoes with dread. One ankle flexed, as if he were getting impatient. *Now or never.*

My fingers scrabbled about, selecting two rocks of medium size — my only weapons. I inched forward on my stomach, crawling up and away from the path at a snail's pace, and when I had gone five feet or so, onto a level stretch, I rose to my feet and began to run as fast as I could away from the path and the sea. My feet thudded against the ground and I knew, without looking, that he was cursing, turning, springing up to pursue me. My legs were weak with terror, and I kept stumbling and falling to my knees. I rolled over, panic-stricken, and lurched up again, running like a mad creature without a destination.

The ocean of gorse seemed to have swallowed me up. I had no idea where I was going and no landmark to guide me. It was as endless as the sea. My breath was coming so hard I was making great gasping sounds, and each gasp ripped through my chest like a knife. Just when I thought my heart would burst, I tripped on a rock and fell, crying out with pain as my knees struck its surface and my ankle twisted under me. I felt warm blood on my leg, and clenched my teeth against the pain. The mist I had prayed for seemed to have obeyed my summons at last, and it drifted aimlessly around me as I stumbled to my feet.

He was directly beneath me. I saw with sick dread that I had come all this way only to wheel around and end up on a hummock just above him. He had been waiting, like a clever hunter flushing a frightened fox, for me to break from my cover. Now, exhausted and limping, I would never be able to escape him. He looked up at me and grinned, the same deadly smile I'd seen that first day on the beach, and then he started toward me.

One of the rocks was still clutched in my hand, as if they were cemented together. I took careful aim and threw it at him as hard as I could, aiming at his head. I missed, but he dodged to the side with a surprised yelp and momentarily lost his footing, and then I was running again, running without looking back. If I'd felt I'd been swallowed in a sea of gorse before, now I was running into a white dream world, trying to hide myself in the very heart of the mist. I prayed for it to grow thicker and conceal me, because soon I'd be able to run no more.

I don't know when I collapsed, panting and exhausted, my hands twisted into the scrub as if it could save me. Time had lost all meaning, and I lay perfectly still, not moving, buried in the drifting fog. Sometimes I heard his footsteps pass by me, and once I was sure he would run right over me, but he was as lost as I was now. The foghorn had begun its deep moaning, and it sounded so close that I had a new fear. What if I had run back toward the sea, and was even now lying on the brink of the cliff? My courage had gone; I couldn't move a muscle.

I was so cold my teeth chattered constantly and my fingers ached. I listened for the sounds of his harsh breathing, but my own breath was rasping so loudly it seemed to blot out everything. I thought it must be night now, for the drifting white world had a darkness behind it more menacing than anything else. Nobody would find me. Nobody knew I had come here. My father would never dream of looking for me here. As for Danny, there had been no loving note from him, no summons to meet him at our special place. He was the only person in the world who would think to look for me here, but Danny didn't even know I was missing. I would lie here throughout the long night, and then, if I hadn't frozen to death, the man would find me in the first rays of the sun.

I thought of my father and of Annie and the new baby on the way, and then of Danny. I said goodbye to them and waited for the long night to be over. Sometimes I thought I heard, very far away, voices calling my name. I knew it was the man, stalking through the fog, calling: Amy! *Aaa-meee!* He hoped to trick me, make me think someone was searching for me, but it wouldn't work.

When I saw the lights beaming through the mist, like fireflies in a hedge on a summer night, I thought I had become delirious. They came closer at one point, and then flickered away in the distance. I closed my eyes and ignored them, but then I heard the voices again. *Amy! Amy!* My frozen fingers convulsed in the underbrush because I knew the voice. It was not a trick, not my tortured brain inventing things.

I tried to call back, to tell my father where I was, but no sound came from my lips. His voice was receding, getting farther and farther away. I struggled to my feet, desperate to make him hear me. My mouth opened on silence again and again. I started to walk toward the sound of his voice, but my legs wouldn't seem to work. *Please, please,* I begged silently, and then I was falling, falling, spinning and turning into that endless airy space that ended in blackness.

Twenty-one

I knew I was in my own bed, and that my father sat beside me, sometimes holding my hand. A doctor came, and I knew then that I'd been very ill. Or had it been a nightmare? My thoughts tumbled in feverish confusion, and then I would plunge into deep, heavy sleep. Whenever I woke up during that long, strange night, my father was there beside me. Once I tried to speak to him, but he laid his fingers gently over my mouth.

"Sleep, Amy," he whispered. "We'll talk tomorrow. You're safe, darling."

In the morning I remembered everything. In some respects it seemed to have all happened a long time ago. I could recall the terror without really remembering what it had felt like. My father brought me orange juice and tea, and held my hand tensely. His face looked haggard, lined. For the first time he looked old to me.

"How did you know where to look for me, Daddy?"

"Are you sure you feel well enough to talk?" he countered anxiously. I nodded. I needed to know. "A private plane flew over the point at about six-thirty," he began. "The pilot noticed something glimmering on the rocks. The setting sun was shining off it, creating a mirror effect. He flew lower and saw that it was a blue bicycle, caught on a rock half-way down the cliff. He radioed in an accident report. I heard it broadcast on the local news, but not until nearly nine o'clock. By then I was sick with worry, anyway. I'd called all your friends, but nobody knew where you were."

I squeezed his hand tightly. I wondered if he knew by now that my would-be murderer had been so confident he'd thrown my bike over the cliffs while I was waiting for Danny. It couldn't have been any other time.

"The police combed the cliff tops for over an hour. I was with them. I knew they thought I was crazy to insist." He shuddered. "They assumed you were lying below on the rocks, but I couldn't give up hope."

"That's what everyone was supposed to think," I said, "and that's where I would have been if . . ." If what? It had all been merest chance that I was alive now. The seabird warning me, the mist coming in time to shield me. The whole town would have assumed that I'd stupidly ridden my bike along those dangerous cliff tops and gone over the side. Another Crozier's Cottage tragedy.

"Daddy, he tried to kill me," I whispered. "A

man — I don't understand why, but it's all connected — "

"He's dead, Amy. He can't ever try to harm you again. He must have still been there when we arrived. He tried to escape by climbing down the cliff. He had equipment; the police think he was something of a mountain climber by the look of it, but in the dark — " My father broke off, and both of us imagined him lying broken on the rocks, where he had intended me to be.

"Who was he?"

"The police would like to talk to you later, if you feel well enough. They'll have some answers for you."

Before the police came, my father told me he held himself responsible for what had happened to me. He held his head in his hands and said if he'd been more aware, less absorbed in himself, he could have prevented it.

"That's not true, Daddy," I said. "I should have told you what I suspected, but I was so confused. Please don't be so hard on yourself." And then, I'm afraid to say, we both cried a little. I felt weak and every muscle in my body ached, but in a strange way I was stronger than my father then.

"You're going to be all right, *sciurus,*" he said. "You're suffering from exposure, and there's a nasty bruise on your knee, but the doctor says you'll be fine."

Two detectives from Klamath visited me later in the morning. It seemed strange to see them sitting in my bedroom, one taking notes while the other politely questioned me. The man who had fallen to his death was named Ernest Patterson. He had been an amateur rock climber, and an ex-convict. He had been released from prison recently after serving eleven years on an armed robbery charge. Patterson had lived in a motel to the north, midway between Klamath and North Point, sharing a cabin with another ex-convict who'd been released at the same time. That man had been taken into custody.

"I saw them," I told the detective. "I saw them on the beach weeks ago. They warned me not to walk there, said it was dangerous."

The detective produced two photographs. "Were these the men you saw?" he asked. My would-be murderer and his friend stared somberly back at me from the mug shots, and I nodded. So far there had been no mention of the third man, but I knew I had to tell the whole truth now.

"There were three of them," I began, and then I told them everything I knew, mentioning the dinghy and the time with the binoculars, reluctantly describing the sketchbook incident, concluding with the note I'd received, and the mistake I had made in answering the summons.

"And the note, Miss Hollis? Who did you think had sent it?"

"A boy named Daniel Morgan. He lives in Klamath. We used to see a lot of each other."

The two detectives exchanged a look. "We've arrested a third man," said the one in charge. He produced another photograph for me. "Is this the third man you saw on the beach?" The face so like Danny's beneath the bitter lines had the power to choke me up. "Yes," I said, turning away.

"Do you know who he is?"

"I'm not sure." Even now, I couldn't bear to say who I thought it was, even though I'd never been more sure.

"His name is David Morgan. I'm afraid he's the father of the boy you mentioned. He was in jail with the other two."

"Do you mean Danny's father committed armed robbery?"

"No. He was a drifter. He's been in and out of jail for ten years, Miss Hollis. He was serving a short term on a check forging rap. He met the other two men inside. They were all released at about the same time."

"What were they doing? What were they looking for at the cliff?"

But the police had evidently decided I'd had enough for one day because they told me it would all come out shortly. They weren't at liberty to make a statement just then. They thanked me and left.

I had one other visitor that day. Late in the afternoon, my father told me another member of the search party had come to see me. "He came the moment I called. He was with me when we found you."

Danny's face was nearly as drawn as my father's had been. He sat quietly next to my bed, his eyes cast downward at the floor. For a long time neither of us said anything, and then I broke the silence.

"Danny? When you broke up with me, was it because your father had come back?"

"Yes. I didn't know what he wanted, but I knew he was up to no good. I didn't want you involved. I didn't want people to say: 'There goes that nice